the LACQUERED CURTAIN *of* BURMA

the LACQUERED CURTAIN *of* BURMA

Eugene Lawrence

olive turtle

NIYOGI BOOKS

Published by
NIYOGI BOOKS
Block D, Building No. 77,
Okhla Industrial Area, Phase-I,
New Delhi-110 020, INDIA
Tel: 91-11-26816301, 26818960
Email: niyogibooks@gmail.com
Website: www.niyogibooksindia.com

Editor: Vibha Chakravarty Kumar
Layout: Shraboni Roy
Cover design: Shraboni Roy and Misha Oberoi

ISBN: 978-93-89136-02-9
Publication: 2019

Printed at: Niyogi Offset Pvt. Ltd., New Delhi, India

I dedicate this work to my parents;
to the memory of my father,
and to my mother, who silently bore the pain of
uproot and sacrifice.

Contents

Preface 9

A Legacy for Aung San **11**

Transcendental Borders 25

The Bridge over the River Khwae Yai **39**

Judson's Converts 69

The General **80**

A Farewell to Rangoon 114

Across the Bay **122**

The Echo from Thailand 131

The Lotus in Rangoon **139**

The Lacquered Curtain 153

Sanda Win **162**

Battle Cry 165

The SLORC **169**

Solomon's Hill 177

Sein Lwin's Salvoes **184**

Mending Fences 208

Change of the Guard **214**

Naypyidaw 219

Acknowledgements 224

Preface

The circumstances and events described in this work have been based on a combination of fact and fiction, and some, close to facts. There has been no attempt to malign personalities or policies of any individual or institution in the portrayal of these events and circumstances. The facts could be easily gleaned by the discerning reader from numerous press reports that have appeared over the past 40 years. While the identities of some personalities could not be altered in the context of the published truth, the identities of some characters have been suppressed, and some are purely fictional. Also, while I have attempted to adhere to facts in the writing of this book, I have taken the liberty to detract from some in order to suit the story.

Having stated that, I wish the people of Myanmar good fortune in resolving the ever-present conflict, and usher in the birth of a democracy free of the oppressed and the oppressor—wherein painful memories can be forgotten, and an era of mutually beneficial coexistence can begin. I certainly include the ethnic people of the land in this environment and wish them an era of peace—long overdue—when they can discard their arms in pursuit of their cultural heritage without fear.

This has left many, including myself, wondering what the future of the diverse nation of Burma will be...

A Legacy for Aung San

A Politician's Residence
Rangoon
Liberated Burma, 1947

The short and savage chapter of Japanese oppression during World War II had ended, and the long history of colonial conquest by the British was at an end. The country was soon to be freed from its shackles of foreign occupation. General Aung San, the legatee of the independence—bequeathed to him by the departing British—had assumed the reins of the provincial government and the responsibility of rebuilding a nation that the war had devastated. Burma was heaving a sigh of relief that the terrible war had ended and the mood of a people had transformed from silent docility to that of eager volubility. Tasting the elixir of freedom, the people now voiced the roles that they would play in the reconstruction of the nation and claim the rewards of riches and recognition.

Audible above the din of the clamorous nation were the shrill and raucous voices of the politicians of the land, and in particular, that of one who was known as the *Garuda*—named after a devouring mythical bird-like creature—more commonly called *Galon* among the Burmese. The entry in Galon's diary on the morning of 19th July that precipitous year indicated that Aung San was to have an important meeting at the secretariat. The general was to present a draft of a new Constitution to his cabinet members that would govern the independent country and make them signatories to implement his policies with the voice of unison. But Galon had a far more pressing matter on his agenda at his residence that morning, which made Aung San's meeting pale in significance. Galon was holding a meeting of his own, albeit covertly, and it was as voluble as it was concerned with the indelible change of the politics of the land.

'Well, my dear comrades,' Galon addressed the group of men who sat with him in secret, 'the time has come for us to put an end to the ambitions of our friend Aung San. He has become the general of the new republic army now and despite of his talk of democracy, I dare say that we will have a fascist amongst us shortly. And we will have only ourselves to blame for want of courage in preventing it.'

'We agree,' said the leader of the group in response.

'Neither the people nor Aung San's ministers realize it yet but by endorsing Aung San, they will be betraying the independence of this country to a demigod,' Galon asserted.

'Yes,' the leader of the group agreed, 'the people worship him as if he is the only one who fought for the independence of this country. They've forgotten the others who have laid down their lives!'

'His photographs are everywhere and it's disgusting to see how he's been idolized!' sneered one of them.

'This worship of him will turn him into a monster and he will enslave the country with his power,' Galon said. 'And when people wake up from their euphoria, it will be too late for they will not be able to confront his army by then.'

'We've had the British and the Japanese yoking us; we don't want our own kind to do the same thing,' the leader of the group declared passionately.

'Precisely,' Galon agreed shrewdly, adding fuel to the fire that was now burning in the patriotism of the men around him.

'Also, we should not underestimate the communists,' said one of the men.

'Yes…absolutely right,' Galon acknowledged promptly. 'They could spring anytime onto the stage with their rather captivating ideology and make things even more calamitous for the country.'

The men who sat in conspiracy with the politician that morning were his most trusted followers and, like him, despised the communists as much as they did Aung San. And like Galon, they were also aware and wary of the emergence of Asian personalities like Mao Tse Tung and Ho Chi Minh, who were indomitably swaying the thinking of a generation of oppressed, and who were putting to question the issue of patriotism beyond their national considerations and borders. With the impending evacuation of the British from their erstwhile colonies and the decline of the French in the Indochina, these new giants of the East certainly made Aung San diminutive in stature, and his ideology, vulnerable. What the group of men sitting with him did not realize then was that beyond the geopolitical considerations of the time, Galon had a personal motive in the denigration of Aung San's ascendance in the country. The general had rudely trampled upon the politician's personal aspiration for power, and had destroyed any opportunity he might have had in the governing of the new republic.

'We'll put a stop to this immediately before he fools the nation with his charisma,' they affirmed their conviction to the delight of the renegade politician.

'Yes, Japanese imperialism is dead and the British Empire is on the wane,' observed the leader of the men. 'It's either us who do the job or the communists will.'

'I have faith in you, my dear comrades,' announced Galon. 'I admire your courage and dedication to the higher ideals we pursue for the country because they are truly democratic, and I foresee

Burman and our ethnic people on the hills sharing a future of peace and tranquillity. The time for *Thakin* Aung San's nationalist prejudice and duplicity is over.'

'We will discharge our duties faithfully,' stated the leader of the group as he turned to look at the men who nodded their heads resolutely. 'Thank you for your confidence in us.'

'Your equipment is in the jeep and will not fail you. It has cost me a tidy sum. So, do use it well,' Galon said. 'Follow the plan accordingly and no harm will come to you. I will get in touch with our allies once you've returned safely.'

The meeting was adjourned and the group of men left the politician's residence in an old rattling jeep to keep their tryst with a destiny that was to change the dream of a leader and his people. Galon watched the car disappear from his driveway and glanced at his watch. Aung San would have just commenced his cabinet session and, within the hour, the politician expected his returns from his little vindictive investment. Galon then turned, immensely pleased with himself, and faced a man in uniform who stepped out agilely from behind the curtain of an adjoining room.

'For a big man, you walk as lightly as a cat,' commented Galon.

'Soft paws usually have sharp claws,' the big man quipped. 'I think a whisky will be just fine?'

'Yes, whisky it shall be,' replied Galon. 'A toast to friends of the hills? I'd rather drink to your end of the bargain, now that I've done mine.'

'So you have,' observed the man, and watched his host who seemed at ease with the familiar uniform of the liberators of the land. It amused Galon that all uniforms were not necessarily loyal to their flags, and that they had minds of their own which sometimes went beyond the call of duty. It was convenient, thought Galon as he filled two glasses with good scotch, that this was just a time.

*

The Secretariat, Rangoon
One Hour Later
19 July 1947

The sky over the capital that morning was clear, with a trace of a wispy white cloud—like a shred of cotton—lacing the stratosphere and changing form from moment to moment over the city by a cajoling wind. It would last for a while before its big brother, the dark gigantic cumulonimbus, in consort with the wind that had lost its patience, would drive it away from the sky and rumble indignantly at the city that had pampered its adolescent brother.

'The union of Burma would not be a true union unless we involve our ethnic peoples in the political, economic, and social process of this nation,' announced Aung San in his opening statement, voicing his vision of an independent Burma to be a union in which all the ethnic groups in the country would be represented by his government.

'I don't believe that we can realize the full potential of this nation unless we open our doors to these people. We must have their elected representatives in our government,' Aung San continued. He was promising an electoral process becoming of a democracy. He had, in 1946, given assurance to the ethnic minorities that, as a people, they would be able to preserve their distinct identity and culture while participating in the development of the nation and equitably share the abundant wealth of the land.

'And unless we do that, this nation will never be able to have any significant or lasting peace and harmony. Remember, the ethnic people are all around us and we can no longer keep them away from claiming their rights to national integration and recognition,' he said.

'Furthermore, we have to bear in mind that the seemingly inhospitable terrain that they occupy is rich in minerals, precious gems and a vast amount of other natural resources that would become unexploitable should we fail to strike an accord with them. But with peace, we can together build a nation of responsible people who will not divert their energies in exacerbating the prejudice and animosity that has existed between us for ages, but work together for the common, mutual good of the nation,' he stated, expressing to the gathering the need to bury the lingering mistrust and hostility latent in the land, and his desire to foster a strong national life for all under his government.

'We have been the dominant people of this land and will remain so, but I ask you: how can we, as a people, prosper when we have to constantly watch our backyard? The army is still young, let me remind you, and it is still a nebulous entity at the moment. And rather than dissipate its potential growth in an attenuating conflict within our borders that will benefit none, I think it will be wise to resolve the differences the ethnic peoples have had with us now and give our *Bamar* people the opportunity to live freely without fear,' he said.

The Burmese were a larger people with a history that had its origins in India, who had settled in the plains of the country, leaving the mountainous regions to the ethnic peoples—many of whom were believed to have inhabited the land prior to the appearance of the Burmese. But, better organized and better positioned for trade and culture and more sophisticated in political evolution, the Burmese had dominated the land over centuries, alienating the diverse ethnic groups in their hill tracks of the west, the fearsome Kachins and red Karens; north-east and east, the war-like Shans, and south-eastern regions of the country where the redoubtable white Karens settled.

The colonial conquest of the British, World War II and the subsequent occupation of the Japanese had removed the lid of isolation off these more predominant of the ethnic peoples, exposing their significance and aspiration to a stake in the country which was on the threshold of independence. Racial distrust, cultural prejudice and the consequent inevitability of alliances that were formed with either of the occupying superior masters —the British or the Japanese—had left a trail of atrocities amongst the indigenous populace in their bid to obliterate the treat of the other, while seeking indemnity of their heritages with either one of the occupying powers.

A man with foresight, Aung San had become sensitive to the needs of these peoples and had come to realize that unless the interests of these people were represented on the national forum, the nation would be besieged with hostilities within most of its borders.

'Once we have settled these issues, we can only look ahead to an era of great wealth, for the land is rich enough for everyone, but I must also warn you that there will be forces in the country, hungry for power, who will try to wrestle from us this opportunity for their own selfish ends,' he declared.

Aung San's colleagues listened with rapt attention, mesmerized as much by the cascading charisma as they were overwhelmed by the truth that was uttered by their leader. A few of them squirmed uncomfortably in their chairs, disturbed by their recent memories of the nationalists' attack on the ethnic communities under the patronage of the occupying Japanese—a backlash to the loyalty of the ethnic communities to the British, particularly the Karens who, apart from helping the British in their three colonial wars against the Burmese, had formed a partnership with Force 136 operating behind Japanese lines with telling effect.

The Karens were formidable; they knew, having had the benefit of rigorous training in guerrilla warfare and with the Japanese gone, that the Karens could now train their guns on their old favourite enemy—the Burmese. Aung San's voice then drifted towards them, parting the screen of thoughts that isolated them individually with their own fears.

'I speak of the communists as well. Regardless of their ideology, their tools speak differently. They speak of terror and violence. They speak of a total power in the hands of a few. They speak of deprivation of individual freedom of thought and the suppression of individual will.

'It is a new kind of enslavement of people and I will not tolerate this happening in our country,' Aung San emphasized. He had closely followed the developments of the curious new emerging force on the Asian continent, politically driven by a fanatical and powerful force that defied any existing ideology that he knew. He himself was swayed by that power in his student days, helping to form the Burmese Communist Party and organizing protests against British colonial rule. But in the Japanese promise of independence from the British and the opportunity of self-governance, the ideology had completely failed to appeal his nationalist determination.

Having braved the gauntlet between the British and the Japanese for the hard-earned reward of independence for his country, Aung San was not ready to enslave his people again in bondage to an ideology that controverted the principles of freedom and self-expression. Independence for the country meant to him the freedom to evolve a system of government suited best to the temperament of its people without importing a new set of masters, whether they are Russian or Chinese. Instead, Aung San was ready to evolve a system that he thought would best embrace the interests of the nation's eager people.

But on that morning, unsuspecting of the evil that hovered in the sky and the ominous howling wind bearing down upon the city, no one paid the slightest of attention to a blue sedan that pulled into the portico of the secretariat. Nor did Aung San have the premonition of the sinister motive of the men who were stealthily climbing the flight of stairs leading to the assembly of men he was addressing that morning. He heard briefly the heavy drops of rain steadily pelting the roof of the building as if in code, warning him of the imminent danger, before the cumulonimbus above burst in outrage and, in a flash of lightning, the assassins crashed into the meeting and discharged thunderously their violent downpour of dissent.

It was a sad day for the young nation, for a curtain had descended upon an incumbent democracy still in its foetal stage. Aung San now lay dead, his body riddled with a score of bullets. And with him died six of his colleagues who were to shoulder the burden to rule a land that he had laboured to set free. A young nation had lost its founding father and hero, and the fledgling army, its beloved general; but a family had lost its head and an important member. A lady was widowed prematurely and a little girl child was to grow up in an environment of independence, deprived of the strength of a father's guidance…and an answer to her consternation that death was the reward for being a hero.

*

Elsewhere in Rangoon

The big guns of the war had fallen silent over Burma, and civilian life was reacquainting itself with the bustling chores of livelihood. After the Japanese defeat in Burma, Immanuel Stanley David, a disbanded soldier of the Indian National Army (INA), had set himself up in the city as a businessman of sorts with a canteen. Paradoxically, he did so with the help of the British, trading in tea and supplying their soldiers with merchandise until evacuation. He entered his canteen that morning, propping his wet umbrella at the doorstep and greeting his manager and trusted assistant, U Maung Shwe.

'Mr David, have you heard the news?' Maung Shwe asked, his voice betraying a sense of urgency.

'What news? I read nothing unusual in the papers this morning,' answered Stanley.

'No, no. Not the papers, the radio,' corrected U Maung Shwe.

'Oh! I'm afraid I've not heard the radio. I hope they've not forecast worse weather,' replied Stanley. 'It's bad as it is. I'm concerned about the tea. We'll have to find better storage soon.'

'It's worse than that, Mr David. They've...they've...some murderers have assassinated General Aung San!' stammered the young manager.

'My God!' Stanley exclaimed. The news shocked him nastily.

'Whilst in a cabinet meeting...shot down like a...about 13 bullets in his body!' Maung Shwe said, choking with emotion.

'Thirteen?' Stanley shivered in disbelief.

'Yes, Mr David,' confirmed the young manager. 'Thirteen. They used Sten guns.'

'This is frightful, U Maung Shwe,' observed a disturbed Stanley.

'How could they do this to him? Our hero...our benefactor...' U Maung Shwe's voice trailed off in consternation. Aung San was his life and his embodiment of self-respect and Burmese pride, as it was to many in the country.

'What now?' Stanley groaned, his mind inundated by frightening visions of chaos and civil strife across the land.

Stanley had pinned his hopes on General Aung San's government to establish Burma as an important member of the British Commonwealth and emerge as a prosperous nation, enabling the likes of him who had shared a common history with the Burmese as subjects of a colonial past, and who had chosen to remain in the country to establish an identity. He had hoped to secure a comfortable livelihood. Stanley had also anticipated an atmosphere of peace and harmony amongst its diverse ethnic peoples. But with the death of Aung San, Stanley was certain that a strong leadership would also die in the nation. He could not see a leader forthcoming in the arena of Burmese politics who could match Aung San's stature.

'The small guns will start now,' he said aloud.

'Yes, Mr David. The ethnic groups will take this opportunity to confront us,' U Maung Shwe postulated in fear. 'They won't trust us.'

'The Karens will fight…that's for certain,' Stanley said without a doubt, now fearing a civil war. He could already hear the chatter of dissenting fire ricocheting in his ears.

The peace had lasted for a short two years from the day the British had released him from the Insein Prison as a prisoner of war, Stanley reflected. It had been a gruelling time for him since 1942, when the war had caught up with him in Malaya, enmeshing him with the Japanese advance that had denied him any volition in his odyssey of the Orient that had culminated in Burma. He had arrived in Burma in a uniform, but with the end of the war, he thought his association with it would be terminated permanently. But now, his troubled mind meandered to the battlefields that lay far away in his mind—to the north of Rangoon—reviving his memories of the conflict that had savaged humanity beyond his comprehension.

*

Burma, 1945

'Take cover! Jump into the ditches!' yelled Captain Stanley David as a menacing flight of three British fighter bombers, like pterodactyls, appeared low over the horizon. The small column of soldiers, elements of the INA, was returning to their camp from an errand in the countryside. The skies over Burma were seeing British aircrafts again after a spell of Japanese dominance, and they were making their sorties with increasing frequency—clawing and plucking Japanese valour off the Burmese skies with their talons of death.

Caught in the open countryside, they dismounted hurriedly from their bicycles; an expedient Japanese innovation for mobility and speed during the War. The men scattered and sought refuge in the shallow craters and ditches along the road. Except for their outdated rifles, they had nothing to defend themselves with—no Japanese anti-aircraft guns puffing the sky in defiance or a Japanese machine gunner trying to pepper the aircraft with bushido contempt as the predators swooped down on them with their lethal wings spread for attack.

They bled from their ears with the rising crescendo of exploding bombs. While some, for a terrifying moment, felt the sharp searing heat of shrapnel knifing through their fragile bodies, shredding life away from them, others gasped their last breath incredulously as staccato bursts of machine-gun bullets tattooed eccentric patterns of death upon them. That some received only merciful showers of dust and stone accentuated the randomness of war in Stanley's mind. He came out alive but injured. A lone stray fragment, hot from a blast, had impacted flatly upon his left shoulder and slid down his arm, peeling away skin till his wrist—a small due he paid as a soldier in the war.

The aircrafts above were on a reconnaissance mission, probing for Japanese strongholds in the path of the advancing army. The raid was merely precursory and had identified a large enemy military base in the area. They had wreaked enough havoc on this run, blasting their machine guns and jettisoning their bomb loads, and were returning to rearm for another mission.

As the flying patrol receded to the horizon, Stanley and the survivors of the attack straggled to the Japanese base. The camp had received full attention from the British pilots and the medical staff was patching the wounded, neglecting the lives that could not be saved and discharging those deemed able to fight another day. For the medical personnel, it was routine that was mounting and becoming difficult to cope with as the months on a frayed calendar leafed over rapidly. The medicine was getting scarcer as most of it was appropriated by Japanese soldiers for themselves, with little left for civilians and the INA soldiers.

Stanley slouched in a corner of a first-aid tent with his arm dressed perfunctorily, and thanked God for the miracle of being alive. He was going to live through this war, he strongly believed now, and thought of the Japanese Army that was losing its belligerence and impetus, and in the process, denuding an aspiring juvenile army of its self-esteem and morale.

This nebulous army had an inherent flaw which was proving fatal, Stanley deduced. It was an army that did not have the nourishment of its native soil, nor did it have the sustenance for self-reliance. For the men, it had depended largely on the Indian soldiers captured in British uniform, numerically small in strength, by the Japanese and on those who had sought livelihood in British colonies. For arms and equipments, it used captured British and Dutch arms initially, and woefully lacked heavy weapons. It depended on Japanese logistics and had no autonomy in planning operation and battle strategy. Although the Japanese high command had a regard for the INA, the ground commanders weren't about to give their best to this unproven army. The INA was thus spawned under this disadvantage, inducting into his ranks Stanley and many like him, who had the misfortune of being caught on the other side of the war.

Stanley, therefore, found himself in Burma now, between an army that was fleeing and an army that was marching towards him. He thought ironically that this kind of perilous wanderlust was not what he had in mind when he had forsaken the safe shores of his motherland, India. But here he was, in another Asian country, a soldier of a vague army, scratched in battle and very likely to be accused as a traitor by the British. He reflected unhappily on how he had become embroiled in this unrelenting circumstance in his life.

It had started with his fascination with the Orient East many years ago.

Transcendental Borders

Calicut (Present-Day Kozhikode), Kerala
South India, 1919

Stanley was born that year into a Christian family converted by German missionaries who worked largely on the coast of Malabar. His father, originally a descendant from the 'Purathu' family, was a Hindu. Deeply moved by Christian teachings, he persuaded his father to let him convert to Christianity. Old Purathu magnanimously allowed him and, there, the name David emerged. Naming himself after the Christian missionary John David, he became John David Purathu. He later changed his name to John Purathu David and began his ministry as J.P. David.

Soon, David needed a church. He approached his father and asked for a small plot of land on which he could build his church. Again, the request was granted by old Purathu. The church was built and David delivered his sermons. All seemed to be going well for the young priest, but soon, Christian zealousness got the better of him. He could not resist the temptation of denouncing the Hindu workers working on his father's land. Forgetting that his father was a Hindu on whose land he had built the church with the same workers, he would brand them as 'Heathens'. The workers tolerated this for a while, but soon complained to old Purathu.

It hurt old Purathu, but in his wisdom and love for his son, he forbade his workers from harming David or his congregation. He said, 'Whenever John talks like that in his sermons, just put up ladders, climb to the roof of the church and start removing the tiles. Let us then see how John delivers his sermons!'

The story was Stanley's favourite and, as he grew older, he became more and more conscious of his Hindu past. He revered his grandfather, for old Purathu was an icon of Christian restraint and tolerance.

At the age of 18, Stanley decided that Calicut was not the place he wanted to be, nor was it a place where he could flourish as a singer. Singapore was, or so he thought. By that time, his eldest sister had established a successful career in Bangalore. She was one of the first graduates of the first women's only medical school in Vellore, founded by Ida Scudder. The school became one of Asia's leading medical institutions of the time.

Stanley travelled to Bangalore and exhausted her with his dreams of Singapore to an extent that she paid his passage to Singapore.

*

Singapore, 1939

It seemed to Stanley that the city beckoned him with a promise of fulfilment. Here was a place where he would emerge as a great singer in the tradition of the Italian masters, and here he would satisfy his curiosity and fascination with the Orient and marry one of his people. As a boy, he had said so to his cousins and friends.

In a few hours, he had managed to lodge himself at The Young Men's Christian Association (YMCA) and, in a few days, he was actively looking for an opportunity in the many dance halls and nightclubs to register his talent. A few songs and a meal in the house were as far as he got, before returning despondently to his room every evening. There was nothing wrong with his voice or his singing; they had just wanted another kind of song. Then one evening, when the money had run out and he was beginning to feel that he was in the wrong place at the wrong time, Frank spoke to him.

'Look Stanley, you've got a great voice, but singing isn't going to feed you anymore,' Frank said in concern.

Frank was Chinese and a new acquaintance in Singapore. A second-generation Christian like Stanley, Frank had received an education in English—the benefits of British colonialism and European Christianity that those so desirous subjects could obtain.

'You need a job, my friend,' Frank advised.

'I can't argue with that, Frank. I guess I'll have to do something else with my voice, huh? But what?' asked Stanley irritably.

'Talk, that's what you can do,' Frank replied after a moment of thought.

'Talk! About what? And who do you think is going to listen to me?' challenged Stanley, and immediately regretted his petulance. Frank was the only friend he had in Singapore, and he had helped him through from the moment he had landed.

'I'm sorry,' apologized Stanley.

'Become a salesman, that's what I was trying to say,' an unoffended Frank said. Fine example of Chinese practicality at its best, Stanley mused.

'As a salesman, you have to talk a lot. Good persuasive talk that, Stanley, you should be able to do,' commented Frank.

Stanley grimaced, seeing his singing aspirations reduced to flotsam by a dawning reality that he would have to do something quickly to survive his misadventure, and that Frank was holding the answer to his predicament.

'I'm not advocating you as a mouthpiece in a shop, Stanley, if that's what you think I'm saying,' continued Frank, sensing that Stanley's spirit was rebelling at the thought of having to surrender his freedom to the mundane task of daily living.

'Freelance…yes, freelance. Look around you. What do you see in this very building? People wearing ties and socks, meaning they are buying them.'

'Make it easier for them. Save them the trouble of having to shop around by getting the goods to them at a fee. In other words, your profit or your income, call it what you like. Add handkerchiefs to your list, so on and so forth.'

'Now, that's a start, but before all that you'll have to locate some reasonable merchants and negotiate a fair price,' Frank explained to an attentive Stanley.

'And if you still want to sing, there's always the church choir, Stanley,' he added smugly with a grin.

A whole new world of possibilities opened to Stanley, filling his mind with anticipation and renewed excitement in his life. He didn't have to return home a failure, at least not yet.

'Frank, you're a genius! Help me find these merchants and I'll get started right away,' declared Stanley exuberantly, already working out portions of his time when he would sell and when he would sing in his mind.

Thus, the two friends busied themselves the next day; one trying to survive and the other, the good Samaritan, doing a good deed which the spirits of his forefathers would have approved. The friendship between Stanley and Frank grew in the years that followed. The small enterprise mushroomed into a sizeable business that sustained the immediate needs of Stanley. He sang bass at the local church and soon became a social entity.

Frank found his way into civil service and became an official of some stature, while Stanley moved into an apartment, establishing an independent existence. He had bought a car that enhanced his area of operation and, after a brisk day's work, had ample time to devote the evenings to new friends and new pursuits, and the occasional stray to the local dance halls. With encouragement from Frank, he began to attend meetings and lectures and heard, for the first time, words from powerful speakers that inspired him. This experience suddenly made his preoccupation with his miniscule world of singing, dancing and selling diminish in significance.

His soul thirsted for knowledge and he quenched that thirst at the local libraries. He read voraciously and finally settled at a fountain from which, however much he drank, he would never be satisfied. Neither his thirst would be quenched, nor the source dry up.

The fountain was mysticism.

Soon, he became the member of a few mystical societies, and became particularly enthralled with Hindu mysticism and philosophy. The Indian mystics fascinated him and, eventually, his mind gravitated to the quest of self-realization and discovering the ultimate reality.

He moved from guru to guru and from society to society, finding the subject of his quest fleeting and elusive, until his spirit began to agitate restlessly. It was then that he realized he needed to be alone, to meditate and to move away from the little nest he had made for himself in Singapore. He was raising a curtain to Malaya, a new environment where he would continue his search alone, and for physical sustenance, he would sign up as a travelling agent with the Australian company for the distribution of potatoes in Malaya that Frank had introduced him to.

*

Malaya (Present-Day Malaysia), 1942

The new job with the Australian company distributing potatoes in Malaya had opened opportunities to Stanley for which his soul had clamoured—opportunity to drive the length of the peninsula from plantation to plantation, giving him the time and space to untie his mind from the clutter of material strife, opportunity to enjoy the verdant expanse of the countryside and live closer to nature, opportunity to meet different people with different temperaments and meditate upon the mystery of the Timeless Being.

The mounting ferocity of the war in the West had merited little of his attention, for it had seemed far removed from his ashram of divine quest. He had exalted himself with serenity and was content with his solitary life when, suddenly, his personal ethereal world of mystical bliss erupted like a volcano with a catastrophic force, shattering his anchor of tranquillity.

The Japanese bombed Pearl Harbor and, with that one presumptuous act, brought a curtain of fire over these parts of the world. The brutal advance of General Tojo's crack assault troops reached Malaya with stunning speed, mauling the hastily retreating Allied Forces with a savagery unparalleled in the recent history of human primitivism—subjugating the local populace with terror in its path.

The grotesqueness of death was evident everywhere his unbelieving eyes looked; the defending rearguard and civilians alike, bombed, strafed, shot or lanced by the bayonet. More horrifying was the macabre sight of headless bodies lying in pools of coagulating blood and victims of summary executions by an indiscriminate and arrogant sword that had shamed the teachings of Zen.

These storm troopers, often led by lowly officers seeking immortality, wouldn't have a reputation less than that of their Teutonic counterparts from barbarity and infamy. They were intent upon proving their martial acumen and determined to patent their superiority in Asia, which tragically made the idea of taking prisoners unappealing to most of these units.

After the carnage came the regular army—warlords in the tradition of the Samurai, tying to restore a semblance of order and propagate an economic hegemony amongst the conquered territories which they called the Greater East Asia Co-Prosperity Sphere. The Japanese Army gained labour, and the populace, slavery. Thc storm troopers had seen to it!

The process of acquisition and confiscation, interrogation and internment, and segregation of the able-bodied for slave labour commenced efficiently amongst the vanquished. It was from this baptism of fear and doom that Stanley surfaced from his cocoon, shaken to the core of his being. He could not understand the acute silence of God over a shocking war that stripped decency and dignity from human beings. War, he now understood, was a far cry from the romanticized notion of uniforms in conflict.

But he had surfaced unscathed, his car untouched and the privacy of his little ashram left inviolated—a miracle that reinforced his belief that divine powers of his maharishi were at work and protecting him from harm. He salvaged what remained of his potatoes and unobtrusively went about bartering for the daily necessities of life.

The Whites who hadn't been killed or imprisoned had since long gone. The Chinese population had been decimated, for a large number of the people had been exterminated as suspected communists or sympathizers, while the Malays had dissolved into their native background like silhouettes in a changing landscape.

The Indians seemed to have survived as a recognizable entity, unmolested by the occupying force. Even those caught alive with British uniforms were just disarmed and interned for a purpose, a design that the Japanese soon intended to stroke on their canvas of conquest. Stanley would shortly become a pigment on this canvas, assuming the form of a singer, but a singer of a different kind of song.

*

A Suburb in Kuala Lumpur, Malayasia

The Japanese canvas of conquest found this pigment in Stanley when he was returning home one evening from the outskirts of Kuala Lumpur. As he neared the city, driving in the dark road, he saw two Oriental men standing by a car and waving him down in urgency. He could not dismiss the uniform they were wearing, for it was Japanese. He also could not ignore the authority of the outstretched hand; it was a command. Stanley pulled over compliantly by their car, praying that this was not a random exercise in violence that the occupation force liked to indulge in, especially after several cups of sake.

'Excuse me, our car has broken down and we need to get to the city immediately. We would be happy to get a lift,' said one of them in flawless English. The politeness surprised Stanley, and he noted that they were officers.

'Of course! At your service,' readily obliged Stanley, relieved that they had not intended to commandeer his car. He got out of his car in a sprightly manner and opened the rear door for the two officers.

The officer who spoke reciprocated with a bow and entered the car promptly with a satisfied smile. The other officer remained silent and unconsciously drummed his fingers on the holster at his waist as he slid into the car beside his compatriot. Noticing this, Stanley decided not to speak while he drove them to their destination. He would just follow instructions and hope they would be satisfied.

'I am Captain Ito and this is Lieutenant Tanaka,' the officer who had spoken earlier said. 'What is your name?'

'Stanley, Stanley David,' answered Stanley amicably, and added quickly, 'I'm from India.'

'Ah! I thought so,' remarked Captain Ito.

'I'm honoured to make the acquaintance of the lieutenant and Captain *San*,' he added, bowing at their reflection in the rear-view mirror. Stanley had learned Japanese courtesy and civility.

'What are you doing in Malaya?' asked Captain Ito. 'You are not a soldier.' It was a pointed question that demanded a forthright answer, and Stanley narrated, though succinctly, the story of how he came to be in Malaya.

'So, you are an adventurer, eh?' remarked Captain Ito. 'But tell me, David *San*,' probed the captain, 'now that there are no more Australians, Americans, or British…or their monopolistic business in this part of the world…for you see, their capitalist stranglehold of Asia is over and Imperial Japan is the power now…what do you think you will do? We don't have potatoes for you to sell.'

Stanley felt his throat constrict slightly while thinking of an answer that would sound reasonable enough to placate the power that could crush him and yet deflect any specific interest in him by the officer. He glanced at the picture of his maharishi that was conspicuously panelled on the dashboard of the car, and drawing comfort from it, answered factually.

'I honestly don't know, Captain *San*.'

'I suppose not,' observed Captain Ito.

Mulling over Stanley's answer, the Japanese captain found it interesting that the Indian—a subject of the imperial British—has not worn their uniform, and felt that the man was probably not a threat to his country's ambitions. Perhaps he could put this Indian to good use, thought Captain Ito. The uneasy silence came to an end shortly when Stanley reached the military camp, where he dropped off the two officers and hoped the acquaintance would end.

'David *San*, where do you live?' Captain Ito asked Stanley. 'Please give me your address.'

The request left Stanley with no recourse but to furnish Captain Ito with his address. The Japanese now knew where he lived. It was only a matter of time, for sooner or later the occupation force would have him account for his presence in the country, Stanley rationalized, and drove away from the camp, thinking nothing of the matter.

The next morning, Stanley received a visit from a Japanese soldier bearing a note from Captain Ito, instructing him to accompany the soldier. Suppressing his instant reaction of fear, he followed the soldier in acquiescence to the camp where he was shown Captain Ito's office. The mandatory picture of the emperor in all his finery took prominence on a wall, while military maps and daily agenda decorated the rest of the office. The office itself was Spartan, noticed Stanley.

'Ah! David *San*, good morning,' greeted Captain Ito heartily, stretching out his hand in a very European handshake.

'Sit down. Have some tea.'

Stanley thanked him and sipped his tea tacitly, and was pleasantly surprised that it was sweet. Sugar was scarce these days, he realized, and wondered why this Japanese officer had summoned him. He looked straight into Captain Ito's eye for an answer without exhibiting any fear, and willing to accept his karma.

'You sent for me, Captain *San*?'

Ito looked at the young Indian sitting in front of him, apparently unafraid of the summon. His name suggested that he was a Christian, but that was probably because of his erstwhile colonial masters. Otherwise, Indians were a mystical lot and this man seemed to bear some of that quality, he sensed. He had noticed the picture of a strange-looking ascetic in the man's car.

'Yes,' he replied. 'Actually, I wanted to thank you for having been helpful yesterday, David *San*,' said Ito, 'because we might have got into trouble.'

The statement was an indication of how popular the invaders were in territories that had come under their occupation. The Japanese Army was not impervious to sudden death at the hands of the resistance, and the more horrifying the reprisals, the more agonizing and degrading the retaliations became. It was human nature to nurture a grudge that, regardless of the might of the oppressor who stripped and outraged what it held sacrosanct, would avenge its rape at every opportunity—however futile or banal it may seem, thought Stanley. Ito was aware that this young Indian had probably saved him and Lieutenant Tanaka from danger, indignity and almost certain death.

'I would like to give you this in appreciation,' he said, and placed a sachet on his desk in front of Stanley. 'It's sugar.'

Stanley was overwhelmed by the gift, for it was more than just a reward. It was his security pass for the moment! He could claim the acquaintance of an officer of the Imperial Japanese Army and would be spared harassment from the ordinary soldier.

'I also have a job for you,' Ito said after a moment, with a wide grin. 'I think you should consider it. This could be your future after Malaya.'

Stanley was astonished for he hadn't expected a proposal, nor was the implicit advice lost on him. He was on Japanese territory, after all, Stanley realized.

'This is wonderful, Captain *San*,' a choiceless Stanley replied. At least, this was better than conscription, he thought.

'But what kind of job?' he asked the captain in curiosity.

'Aaaah!' exhaled Ito. 'It's a bit dangerous, but then there's a war going on and war is always dangerous, and mostly dreadful things happen until finally a good thing can surface.'

'A good thing?' asked Stanley in surprise.

'Yes. The good thing that will emerge is a new world order. A new Asia no longer exploited by the West. Asia for the Asians, with Japan as their guardian and watchdog. What do you think?' baited the captain for contradiction.

Stanley tactfully nodded his head, denoting consent, seeing which the captain elaborated his vision on the new world order.

'Together, we can develop a mighty industrial complex with our resources which the West has plundered all along,' orated an indoctrinated Caption Ito, satisfied for the moment with Stanley's response.

'The bad things we can't help,' shrugged Captain Ito, waving a hand in dismissal, 'are the killings, the suffering, the indiscretion and unscrupulousness of battle troops, some more than the others I concede. But that, I don't have the power to stop. I'm sure every army has its hooligans and its decent men,' proffered the captain.

Was there such a thing as a good soldier or a bad soldier, or for that matter, a good war or a bad one, wondered Stanley, when the semantics of the war spoke only about the taking of life?

Captain Ito rose from his chair and paced the room in deep thought for a while, and then said, 'What I can do is repair the damage and try to minimize the hurt in the memory of the people, for they will be the beneficiaries of the good thing when it occurs. And Japan is fighting this war to bring about this wonderful and much-needed change.'

Stanley listened to the passionate convictions of Captain Ito and wondered whether this military officer was aware of the countless wars that had lost their exalted ideals and floundered upon the maniacal ambitions of glory-seeking generals and callous politicians, indifferent to the abysmal suffering that they were inflicting upon human lives. This was not a moment for philosophical debate, realized Stanley, and continued listening to an impassioned Ito.

'This is the propaganda unit of the Imperial Army,' said Captain Ito, proudly tapping the surface of his desk, 'and our job is to bring this message home to the peoples we have liberated.'

'We need their cooperation. We need them to lay down their arms and eschew their pointless resistance. We will let them work with us to achieve our goals, and we will help them to rebuild and reclaim their independence.'

'I see,' observed Stanley.

Captain Ito looked at Stanley for a moment and wondered whether the Indian sitting in his office really saw or shared his vision of the new world order. He stopped pacing and took his seat, looking at Stanley keenly and waited for a reaction. Lofty ideas, granted Stanley and he asked Ito, 'What exactly would I be doing?'

'We need interpreters to convey our message to the people; mostly yours, Indian soldiers, who had the misfortune of wearing British uniforms. We also need someone to talk to the communists in the jungles,' illuminated the Captain.

'The communists!' baulked Stanley in alarm.

Talking to his countrymen, whatever their uniform, was an agreeable task, but talking to the communists was as good as inviting imminent death, Stanley was convinced. The communists were as fanatical as the Japanese and as unafraid of death as the storm troopers, Stanley knew.

'You will have well-armed escorts, my friend. And, of course, I'll be your guardian,' Ito said in consolation, noticing the obvious distraught displayed by Stanley.

'It will be an adventure and you are an adventurer, aren't you?' Ito challenged.

The truth was that Stanley had no place to escape, nor did he have an alternative. The Japanese had him captive behind their lines, and with that realization he accepted Captain Ito's offer. Thus, a Japanese military officer and he had shaken hands on a delicate partnership that had no common ground. They had journeyed together in a continuum of time, one with illusions of a greater and victorious Japan, and other, a victim of geopolitical circumstance, grasping at an opportunity to survive.

The Bridge over the River Khwae Yai

Around the time that Captain Ito and Stanley, escorted by bayonet-fixed ferocious soldiers, were making their dangerous expeditions into the dense Malay jungles to broadcast Japanese propaganda, another pigment was added to the stroke on the Japanese canvas.

The cry for freedom and independence of a national kind was growing stronger. And there were those who neither had the patience nor the inclination towards non-violence, whose faith in Japanese deliverance made any future British promise dubious. While India had sprung a Bengal tiger who chose not to vegetate on Mahatma Gandhi's non-violent pursuit of independence, Burma saw the emergence of an Aung San.

Seduced like Subhas Chandra Bose by the Japanese propaganda, he championed the cause of his country's independence and, with the typical pride of his people, set forth to claim his entitlement to that Japanese promise. He, too, had envisioned a prominent Burma in the new order of things. The politics were apt, the cause noble and the vision understandable. The Japanese were, in any event, intent upon their capture of Burma in their design for their Greater Far East Co-Prosperity Sphere and take India.

Aung San and his entourage of 30 young lieutenants made their way to the Japanese, crossing the border at Thailand. They were mentored and trained by a Japanese officer called Suzuki Keiji, known better among the 30 as 'Bo Mogyo' (Commander Thunderbolt). Suzuki Keiji was head of a special intelligence unit called 'Minami Kikan', formed to support a national uprising in Burma. Having secured their military training and promise of liberation, they returned to Burma with the Japanese Army.

The force re-entered the country across bridge 227 over the river Khwae Yai. The Japanese built several bridges along the Thai–Burma border between Ban Pong in Thailand and Thanbyuzayat in Burma in 1943 to support its forces logistically in the conquest of Burma, and eventually, India. A quarter million South-East Asian civilian labourers and about 61,000 prisoners of war (PoW) were used for the construction, of which 90,000 civilians and 12,000 Allied prisoners died.

In his entourage was a young lieutenant—a protégé, faithful and astute, who held promise for a future Burma.

His name was Ne Win.

Captain Ito's canvas of a victorious Japan and overlord of the new world order caught fire as the stroke of the brush reached the Imphal pass between Burma and India—its flames slowly and inexorably singeing the cameos of facile conquests as it crackled downwards, taunting the vulnerability of the Japanese Army. Until that moment, the Japanese Army had not really engaged a resolved opponent in equal combat on the battlefield. Determined to teach this Oriental tyrant a lesson in seasoned warfare and exonerate the degradation it had suffered, Field Marshal Sir William Slim's Fourteenth Army began orchestrating its lethal arsenal of war, smelting the Japanese from the landscape that they had been painting.

After the fall of Myitcheena in 1944, the Fourteenth Army's 33rd Corps secured crossings over the Irrawaddy River near Mandalay in January 1945. Late in February, the 7th Indian Division leading IV Corps seized crossings at Nyaungu near Pakokku. The 17th Indian Division and 255th Indian Tank Brigade followed them across and struck Meiktila. Meiktila fell on 1st of March. The town was captured in four days, despite resistance to the last man. By the end of March, the Japanese had suffered heavy casualties and lost most of their artillery, including their chief anti-tank weapon: type 94-37mm gun.

Mandalay fell to 19th Indian Division on 20th March.

The race for Rangoon was on!

*

A Japanese Military Base
193 kilometres North of Rangoon
Burma

The base was a cauldron of fire, its hungry flames fiercely lavishing the combustible material strewn about by the shattering detonations that resounded like violent claps of thunder throughout its perimeters. Dense smoke billowed like pluvial clouds above the base, now littered with the dead. The Japanese anti-aircraft guns had put up strong resistance to no avail as the silver birds flying high above were beyond the reach of their belching, discordant roar.

'Captain sahib!' shouted Sergeant Joginder Singh at Stanley as the cacophony of the guns subsided. The drone of the bombers above had receded with gloating satisfaction at the knowledge that it had inflicted irreparable damage to the enemy who the planes had flown over.

'The Japanese are leaving!'

Stanley looked around and appraised the scene that greeted him. The Japanese were indeed leaving, abandoning their wounded as the rearguard, expecting them to fight to the last and claim immortality in the heavenly abode of their emperor and a god incarnate. This was no longer a proud army with lofty ambitions, he observed. It was a desperate army in rout with no reserves to absorb battle setbacks and regroup as a deterring force. The INA detachments like Stanley's, seeking refuge on their bases, were mostly ignored and left to fend for themselves.

In their grasp for a big slice of the global pie, they had delinquently neglected the logistics essential to keep an over-extended army as a flexible and cohesive force. The prolific industrial response by America to the Pearl Harbor bombing had put back in the Pacific an awesome navy, depriving the armada of Admiral Yamamoto dominance over the sea lanes and disrupting their supply lines extensively.

With the war in the West at an end, the British could now concentrate on their foe without distraction. Compounded by the wrath of a people exacting a pernicious retribution upon them in their backyard, the Japanese fighting capability was soon reduced to suicidal heroics—kamikaze or hara-kiri! The Tanakas of this medieval army chose to ascend to their emperor's heaven, screeching blood-curdling 'Ban Zais' on their dying lips, while the more civilized Itos sought honour in the second.

'*Maa ki Phudi*!' cursed Sergeant Joginder Singh in scatological Punjabi, no longer concerned with propriety. Captain or no captain, theirs was an orphaned army anyway.

This captain was no better off than him, he thought; capture or death awaited both of them.

'*Ye Japaani aadmi mein lund nahi hei kya*!' he wailed derisively, not being able to help the profanity. To him, the Japanese Army had lost its rapacity—a penis that was fast shrinking and, along with it, bastardizing his dreams of taking up a position in a new India!

Another spectre of a more frightening nature hovered over him, for in his mind's eye he could see his fellow sardars, a proud warrior lot of the British Indian Army, marching triumphantly towards them.

'*Mera gaand phutti gaaye*,' he moaned, feeling terribly denuded.

Stanley chuckled at the litany pouring out of the sardar's heart and left the sergeant to worry about the sanctity of his posterior as he mused upon an insouciant kaleidoscope of time. He and his unit were caught in a war at the wrong time with the wrong army, wearing the wrong uniform and were to be wronged for the wrong reason, he thought dejectedly. God would understand, he mused, but would the British?

The question whirled in his mind, toiling for a palatable answer but found none. He was, however, relived that the Japanese wouldn't be the judges; the British would, and he expected that they would be more civilized in the treatment of their captives.

'Sergeant!' he barked, asserting his authority as he recovered from his thoughts.

'Gather the men immediately,' he ordered, 'I have a plan.' The fires had died and the smoke cleared, unveiling the wreckage of machine and men the aerial assault had caused.

Diligently, Sergeant Joginder gathered the handful of men around Stanley; men who had been defeated twice by two different armies in a short span of three years, men whose spirits were shaken by the mocking cry of irony.

'I know many of you are thinking of desertion,' he said, 'but deserters forfeit any respect that might be accorded to them by any army.'

'Then what are we to do?' demanded the demoralized soldiers, staring at Stanley with disbelief.

'Fighting the British is senseless,' one of them declared.

'And for who?' asked another scornfully. 'For the Japanese?'

'No,' Stanley said. 'We will not fight. We don't have to.'

'This is our only chance,' implored the sergeant, 'before the Japanese themselves have fled and there is no one to shoot us for desertion,' he reasoned.

Stanley stood calmly, cognizant of the soldiers' dilemma and raised his hand to gain their attention.

'Are we combat soldiers?' he asked argumentatively. 'Have we killed a single British soldier? The others have, but we haven't. Yes, we are in the INA, but the arms we bear are for defence only,' Stanley argued with the sudden lucidity of a desperate mind.

'We are a propaganda unit and the greatest crime we are guilty of is talk; talk that hasn't actually incited a mass revolt amongst our countrymen on the other side,' he added.

Sergeant Joginder Singh and the men around Stanley gaped at their officer, wondering what the captain was driving at. Immediate escape in the absence of the Japanese appealed to them the most.

'What are you trying to tell us, Captain?' asked the sergeant. 'I'm afraid we don't understand.'

'Very well, I'll come to the point,' replied Stanley.

'Where do you think we can escape? You're not following the Japanese, right?'

'That's right,' answered a soldier affirmatively.

'Which means that you plan to hide amongst the civilians and take your chances.'

'Yes,' confessed a soldier.

'So far so good, but I don't believe that you can get very far on your own. Don't forget the Burmese. To them, we're all part of the Japanese Army. We don't have an ally…even Aung San has crossed over to the British. They'll kill us as readily if they get hold of us,' warned Stanley.

Stanley was not certain if they would be able to elude the British until the end of the war, nor had he reason to believe that they could survive in hiding individually amongst the people, considering that the chaos would soon precipitate indiscriminate killings by an avenging indigenous population.

'But as a group holding onto our arms, we will have better odds at survival,' Stanley said.

The group of men around Stanley fell silent and began to balance the odds of surviving the war. What the officer said made sense, especially regarding vengeance-seeking vigilantes of the land waiting in the wings to settle their grievances, but they were hesitant and undecided on surrendering their immediate freedom to whatever plan their officer had.

'My plan is to fall back a little where the Japanese have left and take control of it until we reach Rangoon. They had heard that their leader, the Bengal Tiger, was dead, along with a Japanese general Tsunamasa Shidei in an air crash a week ago while retreating from Rangoon before its imminent fall to the British.

'Colonel Loganathan and his men should be there. I doubt the Japanese would still be around,' Stanley argued, explaining his plan to the soldiers, but aware of possible mutiny fermenting in the minds of his partners in misfortune.

'We will police the area until the British arrive, and then surrender. We could be seen as a lot discharging a worthy duty in the face of defeat.'

It was evident to the men that the disorderly retreat of the Japanese Army was creating a backlash in the areas that they had vacated, which were now devoid of law and order—a vacuum which was getting filled with a native enterprise of loot and plunder, with little regard to life and property. Aung San was yet to appear with a police force.

'We will ask for fair treatment according to the Geneva Convention, for we are still soldiers in uniform,' he promised his men.

'The British will take us in as PoW, which is better than getting shot or ill-treated as deserters.'

'Now, who will join me?' Stanley demanded, intuiting in the vacillation of his men, an opportunity for his own survival and the fulfilment of his obligation to his men as an officer.

His sudden forceful call for a consensus hastened his men to reckon with the perceptible facts of the moment. Being foreigners in a country that was in the grip of anarchy, they too realized that they were safer together as a group. Rather than risk an individual attempt at escape with a very likely certainty of being apprehended and slaughtered by a volatile mob, they decided to entrust him with their lives.

*

About 105 kilometres from Rangoon

Stanley and his band of eight men fell back a little before Rangoon—steering clear of the populace—and occupied a small school, long desolated. It was, however, adequate for their shelter until the British came. Scouring the countryside for sustenance, meagre as it was, they began to discharge their responsibilities as policemen—albeit without sovereign authority, in the few weeks of freedom that lay ahead of them.

The countryside was indeed infested with dacoits and looters; unsavoury elements of the land, armed with indigenous weaponry and an occasional scavenged gun, who preyed on the refugees of war now disoriented by a changing tide of power foreign to them. With deplorable disregard for human life, these bandits and looters butchered and plundered their way through the only possessions of menial value that the helpless refugees carted or carried on their backs.

Appearing to be armed more sophisticatedly than most of the looters, Stanley and his sullen band actually sported a few British Three-O-Threes and obsolete Japanese single shot rifles. Between the nine of them, they shared the only Sten gun and were dangerously low on ammunition. Despite being inadequately armed, they patrolled the neighbourhood, and the few weeks of policing were not without encounter and peril for Stanley and his motley army. But nobility had a way of wearing a hero's garb, and it was one such encounter that would remain etched in the memory of his nondescript army.

'Captain sahib!' yelled Sergeant Joginder Singh when he saw a convoy of refugees ahead of him as they went on one of their morning scouts. He reined the pony cart, which was their transport, to a standstill, and shouted, 'Looters! *Dekho*....*Dekho*!'

Stanley appraised the situation and, in an instant, realized that a looting in its early stages was in progress. The looters didn't seem to possess a gun, he noticed with great relief, but they outnumbered his strength; he had brought only three of his men today, leaving the rest at the school.

The Sten with them, however, bolstered his morale and encouraged Stanley to draw closer to the convoy of refugees. Grabbing a rifle at random, he jumped out of the cart with a command.

'Sergeant! Stay with the men and cover me.'

The men were nervous at being outnumbered, but the command of their officer prompted them to obey, and they quickly brought their weapons to a state of readiness.

'Stop!' commanded Stanley in a deep voice, bolting his rifle and aiming it at the man who appeared to be the leader of the bandits.

It was the leader. Tall and tanned by a marauding sun, this man was hefty and wielded in his massive hands an obnoxious *daah*, a deadly native sword that could cleave through flesh and bone without a smirk. But this was a *daah* that had truncated less of Japanese limbs than it had savaged many an unarmed refugee.

'*Kway Kalaa*!' the leader swore as he turned and stared into the barrel of Stanley's rifle.

'Drop the *daah* and tell your men to lay down their weapons.... Now!' Stanley barked, steadying his aim and summoning all his will to remain bold, ignoring the stinging insult of being called an Indian dog by the snarling Burmese bandit.

He realized at that moment that he had every reason to fear for his life. The damned rifle was not loaded! Some idiot's carelessness and his own lapse were going to cost him his life. 'Damn!' he cursed, and felt mortified. The bandit leader did not drop his *daah* but stared at Stanley with loathing. He firmly griped the *daah*, and poised truculently for a sweeping strike. For a long moment, the tall Burman gauged the possible outcome of a conflict despite the cold glare of the rifle. He wanted to murder this Indian but the bastard had the gun in his hands, and so had the other dogs in the cart, he accepted with bitterness.

'Drop the *daah* now or I will shoot!' ordered Stanley, staring resolutely back at the Burman, his mind furiously calculating the arc the slashing *daah* would take. It was time for another miracle, Stanley thought ruefully, and wondered whether he was running out of his share when the bandit leader dropped his *daah*. Martyrdom wasn't his cup of tea, decided the leader and spat on the ground. He would leave that to the Aung Sans of the country, he thought, and signalled to his men to discard their weapons. The bandits retreated and soon, like evil gnomes, seeped into the porous countryside.

For the refugees, it was a moment of salvation and their gratitude, though enormous, could only be expressed in frugal terms. Rice, salt, tea and some dried fish were given as a gift to the soldiers which, to Stanley, were reassuring promises of the essential goodness of mankind. They returned to the school, the good deed of the day done, and prepared a meal for themselves. Each thought of the morrow and the day after, and waited for the British to come.

*

A Burmese Village near Stanley's Camp

It was on a Sunday morning, when waiting for the British who seemed still distant, that Stanley had a craving for meat and announced his welling appetite for a sumptuous meal to his men.

'Let us go and get a goat…' Stanley's announcement wasn't over yet when he realized that the sergeant and a few of the men had scrambled to their cart and were waiting for him with expectancy. None of them had had a decent meal in what seemed an eternity, and the mouth-watering aroma of a mutton curry captivated their imagination and galvanized the men into action. There would be no problem following the leader this time, Stanley thought, amused at the scene.

'Where to, Sahib?' asked the driver of the cart, his yellowing teeth flashing in a wide grin.

'There's a village nearby,' Stanley said. 'We will go there and try to buy a goat,' he proposed, pulling out some crumpled currency which was the sole wealth he had managed to acquire until now.

'*Theek hai*, Sahib,' gleefully acknowledged the driver, jerking the reins of the pony as the animal laboured for another day's mournful clop.

The pony looked as emaciated as the men it was carting about, Stanley noted, and reminded his men to gather some fodder for the animal while looking for his goat. They arrived at the village shortly after and alighted from the cart, surveying it for any hostile elements.

'Are your rifles loaded?' he asked his men, making sure that his was. He did not forget the recent lesson he had learnt. The men nodded in affirmative and felt remorse; they had come close to losing this officer last time, a man on whom they had depended for their survival.

Stanley stopped at the village square and assumed a benign posture, not wanting to antagonize or frighten the villagers. He saw chickens, ducks, geese and pigs—all cackling, quacking, hissing and grunting about their day, leaving the worries of the war to their owners. Time for them was the division of day and night; life was when the blood circulated in them and death was when it stopped. Stanley marvelled at the simplicity of their existence which did not carry the burden of memories or the anguish of the future.

Stanley looked for a goat, and found a few some huts away. He approached a hut, calling out for its tenants. He stopped a short distance away from it when no one came out. By now, the villagers had begun to gather around, watching the armed men invading their village. Stanley cautioned his men to be alert.

'I want a goat for my men,' he spoke in an amiable voice, pointing to a stout billy goat that his eyes had chosen for food.

'We are very hungry and haven't eaten for days,' he explained, gesticulating as he spoke, hoping that his message would be understood by the villagers.

The villagers watched him in silence as he made gestures of feeding himself and patting his stomach. They comprehended Stanley's meaning but also eyed the rifle in the other hand with distrust, mostly with rebuke, for he was not one of their kind; he was a soldier, and they had come to revile soldiers these past years.

'We will pay for the goat!' assured Stanley, pulling out his currency and showing it to the villagers. 'Who is the owner of that goat?' he asked, pointing at the one he had selected.

The villagers remained scornfully silent and watched the drama that was unfolding before them. Some of the children clung to their parents in fear, while some actually smiled, innocent of the temper of the village, Stanley saw, and was moved with a profound sorrow for the children. These were little hands that should be clapping and little voices singing with joy, he thought, and not threatened by the banality of war.

'Please,' he entreated the villagers again, 'we mean no harm. We just want a goat,' he said.

The villagers were adamant in denying him his need and dared him with their silence.

Stanley raised three fingers in exasperation and said, 'I will count till there.'

He then targeted the goat with his rifle and patiently curled an impelled finger around the trigger of his rifle.

'At the count of three, if no one comes forward to claim the goat, I will shoot it,' he issued an ultimatum, trying not to let his anger edge into his voice. His ultimatum elicited no response from the villages except an involuntary flinch when the sharp report of a single shot from his rifle reverberated throughout the village.

Stanley had his goat.

*

It had been some time since Stanley and his men relished a stomach-filling meal and indulged themselves voraciously on it. The meat was succulent and as they ate, an atmosphere of contentment settled amongst the men. They looked at Stanley and, for the first time, a feeling of brotherhood overwhelmed them. From resentment to reason and dependence to comradeship, their short journey had taken them. They now felt forlorn that their journey was coming to an end.

'Captain sahib,' the sergeant looked at Stanley and enquired, 'what do you plan to do after the war?'

Still chewing on a piece of mutton, Stanley considered the question. The wistful thought had been on his mind.

'I don't know,' he replied dolefully. 'Malaya would probably never be the same…and…'

'Don't you want to go back to India?' interrupted one of them in surprise.

Shaking his head almost imperceptibly, he answered, 'I'll stay on in Rangoon for a while and then decide.'

'Do you think Gandhi will get the independence for India?' asked one of the men eagerly.

'I don't know,' Stanley replied, shaking his head. 'But I know something,' he said and paused for a moment to chew on a piece of mutton.

'This war will change many things, my friends,' Stanley continued. 'I think or at least hope that people will get tired of killing people and want to live peacefully for a long time to come.'

Like his men, Stanley, too, wished an end to the violent forces of destruction and the killing that stupefied him. He hoped that the period of rebuilding ahead by almost all nations on the globe would necessitate an environment of compromise and rapprochement that would prevent the firing of guns by men in a millennium. He was not to know then that man's ideologies had irrevocably acquired the taste of power with the knowledge that no other statement of power spoke better than that spoken from the barrel of a gun.

*

Stanley's Camp
April 1945

Two days later, an advancing patrol from the vanguard of Field Marshal Sir William Slim's army was sighted from the roof of the school by a vigilant Sergeant Joginder Singh.

'Captain sahib,' he called out anxiously, 'the British are here!'

Stanley's leg sprang into action on hearing the sergeant's call. There was no time to be lost. He bounded to the lone mast still standing in the school yard.

'Get the flag!' he shouted, indicating at the piece of rag they had preserved for the occasion.

The men hurriedly hoisted their flag of surrender on the mast and gathered around with their weapons, awaiting further instructions from Stanley.

'All right, my friends,' he said. 'We have been waiting for this moment and we're ready for it. Fall in now and remember, I'll do the talking and I want everyone to be calm,' he reminded them and instructed them to lay down their weapons in front of them.

'Don't worry, everything will go well,' he reassured them.

Each of them felt ridiculous about their charade and suppressed the swelling doubt and fear that tugged at their hearts. They accepted that they were now past the moment of choice and left their moment of reckoning in their captain's, the British and God's hands. Stanley hoped he was right, looking at the group of men who had placed their faith in him, and silently prayed.

'At-ten-tion!' he commanded his men as soon as he saw the patrol moving into the premises, bringing his men and himself into a prefect military posture. The patrol kept their distance, covering Stanley and his men with their weapons—wary of a possible ambush, and surveyed the picture before them. They were surprised at the theatrics but mostly relieved that the men before them were not Japanese!

It was important to Stanley how he and his men would be regarded at that moment, for, on that would depend the treatment they would receive ahead of them. He saw a good number of his countrymen on the other side, and a few of the British who looked a bit nonplussed. Stanley's apprehensive eye was searching for an officer. He identified in an instant a young British lieutenant gripping his service revolver adroitly in his hand.

'We are a non-combatant unit of the INA,' Stanley spoke aloud, expecting to gain the attention of the officer.

'We have been in the school and have secured the area for a few weeks, and have been waiting for you. We wish to surrender to you,' he announced resonantly.

'Bloody hell!' Corporal Brown exclaimed. 'The bloke's speaking in English!'

Stanley heard that, satisfied with the response and stifled a desire to laugh, for it always amazed him to see the startled reaction of a white man when spoken to with proper English by a coloured man. They probably believed seriously that God was an Englishman and that they were the only ones privileged to speak the tongue. They didn't seem to have a problem with the Pidgin English that sprouted in their colonies; they were delighted and patronizing about it, for it probably affirmed their sense of superiority, thought Stanley.

'There are no Japanese for miles around and you'll probably see them only in Rangoon if you hurry!' he reported, and remained in rigid attention.

'Lieutenant?' Corporal Brown enquired. 'Frankly sir, we should go in and kick their butts, if you ask me,' advised the corporal quietly into the ears of Lieutenant Murray. Corporal Brown was not without animosity, for he had seen many of his mates falling to enemy bullets in the north of Burma, and during the taking of Mandalay Hill. Anyone with the wrong uniform, to his uncomplicated mind, was simply an enemy. It didn't matter to him that it was a young Indian major, who was in the lead assault on the hill.

'Easy, Corporal,' Lieutenant Murray restrained Corporal Brown. Invested with the more complex responsibility of an officer, the lieutenant was unsusceptible to the diatribe of Corporal Brown. The British Army, the lieutenant believed, was not about fighting one man's personal derision of the enemy, but was here to reclaim a glory that the Japanese had defiled, and to demonstrate that it was a civilized army unlike that of their foe.

'Sorry, Lieutenant,' muttered the corporal, 'just voicing an opinion, sir.'

'I understand,' condescended the lieutenant. 'They're INA and not Japanese; we have our strict orders where these chaps are concerned, Corporal.'

'I'm Captain David and these are my men. I request acceptance of our surrender immediately, and to be treated accordingly as prisoners of war,' Stanley demanded firmly, fixing his eyes on the lieutenant.

With the revolver back in its holster, Lieutenant Murray strode across the yard towards Stanley and his men, scrutinizing each of them and, finally looking at Stanley, curtly saluted the captain. This man has a sense of protocol and appears civilized, he inferred, and was returning the compliment. They could have hidden themselves in the building and waved their pathetic rag, but instead chose to parade themselves in surrender. The honour pleased him.

'At ease, Captain…your men as well,' he ordered and extended a formal hand. 'Lieutenant Murray. David…did you say your name was?'

'Stanley David, Lieutenant Murray,' replied Stanley over the stiff handshake.

'I will send you and your men with guard as my prisoners for interrogation to Division Headquarters, Captain David, but beyond that, it's up to the chaps there,' Lieutenant Murray said.

'I completely understand, Lieutenant,' replied Stanley, heaving a sigh of relief.

'Which unit are you chaps from, Captain?' enquired the lieutenant, with a scrutinizing look on his face.

'Propaganda, second division, 4th regiment, Lieutenant,' answered Stanley.

'Oh! I see,' observed the lieutenant. 'Haven't had much of a score with your lads on our side of the war, have you?'

'I guess not,' acknowledged Stanley.

'Curious, isn't it?' remarked Lieutenant Murray, looking at Stanley again. 'How'd you get into that uniform…but I suppose you have a story for Division Headquarters, right?'

'Not a very exciting one, I'm afraid, but I'm glad it's over,' replied Stanley graciously.

'Anyway, Captain David, good luck to you!'

With an army on the march that had little to lose in the capture of the Japanese in Rangoon, Stanley found himself moving behind the vanguard of the British Indian Army towards the city. Rangoon fell, and with the fall, the British could now quarantine their captives securely. For the first time in his life, Stanley saw the insides of a jail—a jail that had seen change of guard and wardens three times in the tug of war.

It was the dreaded Insein Prison, a prison that would incarcerate and punish the criminals amongst the society, or silence the conscientious voice of dissent in the decades ahead, satiating its enormous appetite with variety. But for that moment, Stanley was a morsel, fed into its gullet and ingested without choice—its taste or value yet to be determined and processed by a stomach suffering from the early symptoms of indigestion. The prison was full. The singer, salesman, propaganda soldier was now a prisoner of war.

*

Insein Prison
Rangoon, Burma

The British Army was back in Burma, a country whose population wasn't too keen on their presence but accepted it as lesser evil. The resentment to colonial rule had incubated an Aung San, until an opportune moment when he had led a delegation of trusted aides to the Japanese. But Aung San, to his dismay, had soon seen the insidiousness of the Japanese and the fallacy of their promise. Their atrocious disregard of the alliance and the dehumanization of his countrymen angered Aung San. He then realized that the independence of his country actually lay in the hands of the British!

An inspired man filled with political acumen, Aung San and his entourage eluded their liberators-turned-captors and had, in the dense northern jungles of Burma, met with the field marshal. Aung San had risked being shot for treason. With total disregard for his life, he had displayed remarkable courage and self-sacrifice, and demanded of the British the independence of his beloved land. His single-mindedness and dedication to his country had earned him the respect of the field marshal, who did not shoot him; Aung San was given the assurance of consideration of his country's independence. In turn, Aung San was to support the Fourteenth Army with his reformed Burma Independence Army.

And there was the matter of Gandhi in India, who was making a definite impact on British political thinking that the independence of India was assuredly only a matter of time. The INA was an embarrassment to Gandhi's efforts, but also sensitive for the Indian masses. It was a delicate situation for the British. Those were the thoughts ruminating in the mind of Colonel MacIntyre, sitting at the desk in Insein Prison, when he glumly looked at the task ahead of him—to process speedily the matter of the prisoners of war before the army continued its pursuit of the Japanese defeat.

'Fetch me this fellow,' he ordered an attendant, and tossed a dossier on his desk. The dossier was marked:

Immanuel Stanley David
Rank of Captain
Indian National Army, Propaganda Unit
4th Regiment, Second Division

'One of Bose's boys or that Shah Nawaz chap,' he remarked with a yawn, wondering how the devil this army had ever come about.

'Not an acquaintance of the Tokyo Rose, are you now? Being a propagandist and all!' drawled the colonel, laughing at his little joke when Stanley was seated before him.

'What the devil did you think you were doing with those abominable Japanese?' thundered Colonel MacIntyre, quite infuriated with the notion that the INA had entertained the thought that they could actually take on the British!

Stanley realized that the colonel was not addressing him singly but as a collective whole, and wondered whether the allusion to the Tokyo Rose would augur the serious charge of sedition.

'Pardon me saying so, sir,' Stanley replied with equanimity, 'the Indian National Army was just an expression of a sentiment that is becoming popular in these times, foolish as it may have seemed…but speaking for myself.' Then he followed through, 'I have nothing against the British except their colonial policy, and personally, I think they are better gentlemen than most I have seen.'

'Humph.' Stanley's experience of the Oriental warlords had not been exactly endearing, and the remark provoked the grunt from the colonel. 'Loser's tale, eh?'

'Not quite, Colonel,' responded Stanley in defence. 'I'm sorry if I have sounded patronizing, sir, but the truth is that we are also human beings and naturally, as human beings, we desire freedom and dignity even if we are not considered as equals.'

'I say!' exclaimed Colonel MacIntyre, raising his bushy eyebrows as he stared at Stanley and blurted aloud. 'Another bloody patriot!'

Stanley hoped that he had not antagonized the colonel's sensibilities. Stanley knew that this man had the authority to be lenient, and that he and his men could become mere files to languish in the morass of army bureaucracy. 'I speak for my men and I, sir. The truth is that none of us were ever combatants. We were writers of stories some read.'

Stanley had presented his case.

Colonel MacIntyre accepted Stanley's argument without comment. Being well attuned to the tide of change in human thinking and having fought across two continents for the very ideals of freedom from tyranny, his attitude had dramatically changed from those of the old colonial school of thought. A thoughtful silence permeated the room as the colonel perused Stanley's file with great intent, contemplating the scanty material it held, before he broke the silence.

'So I see. So I see,' he observed.

'I meant no disrespect or offence when I spoke about freedom or dignity, Colonel. I was appealing,' said Stanley ingratiatingly, and looked into the colonel's eyes for the judgement that was slowly taking form.

'I say, old chap, point taken,' said Colonel MacIntyre. 'You chaps are getting your independence, no bother. And so are the blokes in this country. It's only a matter of time. I only hope you know what to do with it. But that shouldn't be my concern, should it?' chided the colonel in exasperation.

A curtain was descending upon the British Empire, he surmised. The political process was changing. Britain was spent after years of fighting, and there were the Japanese to contend with still. His job here was to weed out the dangerous elements among the captives and release the rest as a legacy for the nebulous governments shaping on the horizon to inherit. He suspended his train of thought and expelled his decision.

'Mr David,' Colonel MacIntyre said. 'You and your men can consider yourselves no longer under charge of the British Army. You are free to go,' he concluded, stamping the papers in front of him with a rubber stamp.

'Thank you, sire,' gratefully acknowledged Stanley as the colonel stamped him 'NOT DANGEROUS'. Stanley was given the white card.

Nodding politely at the colonel, Stanley walked out of the Insein Prison after an internment of three months with nothing in his pocket but an exhilaration of joy, the joy of being alive and unchained from the war. He was a free man again, free to explore Burma and discover its quintessence without the yoke of a uniform. He was eager to see what a war-free independent Burma would be like, and perhaps pursue and realize the fulfilment of his Asian dream—a dream that had eluded him until now.

*

Aboard HMS Birmingham
Rangoon Harbour
4 January 1948

The captain of the British cruiser anchored in the harbour looked at his watch. Exactly 4:20 am, he recorded, as expected of him by the Burmese astrologers, he gave the curt order.

'Fire!'

The guns from the British warship along with UBS May Yu—a war ship gifted to independent Burma by the departing British—boomed, the crash of the salvos ringing in the ears of the citizenry of the city as they rose to the occasion and cheered. They cheered because the foreign naval guns were not firing upon them for once in their recent lifetime. The British guns were instead officially signalling and confirming to them that they were now free. At the secretariat, diplomats and Burmese officials commenced their ceremony for the momentous occasion. The British Union Jack was lowered and the national flag of the country was hoisted as star shells burst above, awakening a drowsy sky. Rifle volleys were fired by the jubilant Burmese soldiers of the new republic. The much-cherished dream of Aung San had become a reality, and with it would also follow what the general had feared.

*

Rangoon
31 January 1949
The Insurrection

The assassination of General Aung San triggered in the country an aftermath of militancy. And as feared by Stanley and his manager and assistant U Maung Shwe, soon the ethnic communities—in particular the Karens—distrustful of Burmese intentions as ever, withdrew from the dialogue, demanding independence. They were ready to carry arms in order to achieve their objective.

The Karen National Union (also known as KNU) was created as a governmental presence for the Karen people in 1947. It created its armed wing, the Karen National Liberation Army (KNLA), to provide security to refugees or internally displaced Karens. The KNLA attempted to co-exist peacefully with the Burmese majority. Meanwhile, a more aggressive fighting element was formed, veterans of the war, the Karen National Defence Organisation (KNDO). The KNDO prepared for a total uprising. Towards the end of the rainy season in 1948, the Burmese government, led by Prime Minister U Nu, began raising and arming irregular political militias known as the *Sitwundan.* These militias were under the command of Ne Win, a major general by then but outside the control of the regular army. The *Sitwundan* was to disarm the Karens, but some of these militias went on a rampage through Karen communities.

The burning, killing, looting and raping of a people had commenced with sovereign right for the British government of Clement Attlee in their haste to decolonize an empire that was no longer manageable; had disastrously overlooked the need to provide safeguards for their erstwhile loyal subjects and comrades in arms.

Even then, the Karens held leading positions in both the government and the army. The army chief was General Smith Dun. In January 1949, Dun, a Karen, was removed from office and imprisoned. He was replaced with Ne Win by Prime Minister U Nu.

The KNDO rose up in an insurgency against the government and came close to capturing Rangoon itself. The most decisive was the Battle of Insein, nine miles from Rangoon.

*

The Ambush at WetKaw
The End of Karen Ascendance
1 February 1949

While the experienced 5th Burma Rifles stationed in Arakan was being airlifted on the orders of General Ne Win, the Second Karen Rifles—the best equipped battalion of the Karen army of the government—rushed down from Prome to strengthen Karen defences at Insein. An armoured carrier spearheaded 120 vehicles supported by two six-pounder artillery pieces and eight three-inch mortars. On the Burmese side, a six-pounder gun crew and a Naval Bofors gun crew were hastily organized to provide artillery support. In the early morning of 10 February, the mechanized force of the Second Karen Rifles crossed Wetkaw bridge at leisure and commenced to make a dash for Rangoon, feeling invincible and fully confident that there were no government forces or guns strong enough to oppose them all the way to Insein. Fortunately for the government forces, the element of surprise was with them. The Bofors gun mounted on wheels—which was capable of firing 40-mm shells at 120 rounds a minute—stood on the road in their way and opened fire point-blank at 500 yards, knocking out their armoured carrier and damaging one of the six pounder guns.

This was totally unexpected by the Karens who neglected to position a scouting patrol in front. For the next few days there were attacks and counter-attacks, and exchanges of mortar fire between the two forces until the Bofors found clear Karen targets. This demoralized the Karens. Then Nehru's government shipped arms to the Burmese Army. It was the end of the most crucial phase of the Karen struggle. It was a display of remarkable military capability of the Karens as a fighting force but, sadly, without a disciplined command structure. Yet, they held out in a siege till late May 1949 lasting 112 days.

And along with Aung San's dream of a unified Burma, Stanley's stock of tea, valued at 50,000 rupees—considered a fortune then—went up in smoke during the insurrection.

Stanley saw Aung San's Burma deteriorate into a quagmire of political bickering. Diverse political parties sprouted in the country with dangerous portent, while insurgencies, endemic to the countryside, were beginning to assume cult proportions amongst the ethnic young. Despite the disquiet that had ruptured in the country, Stanley was still hopeful that the nation would find an answer to its problem and iron out its differences, giving him the opportunity to establish an identity in a land to which he had become attached.

Dispossessed now of a business and a means of livelihood in a country where he had decided to remain, Stanley now looked for a job.

He wasn't quitting Rangoon just yet.

*

A Railway Station
Southern Burma

With a semblance of order restored in Rangoon, U Nu's inchoate government pursued an ineffective policy of appeasement with the ethnic groups, successful with some but largely unsuccessful with the defiant Karens. But there were those who chose to be assimilated into mainstream life—abandoning their austere habitat on the hills and descending onto the plains below, forming little hamlets and villages behind the line of control to live with the Burmese peacefully. Many of them educated themselves and sought jobs in Rangoon. However, a majority of the Karens remained on their hill tracks, bordering Thailand, staking their claim to an autonomous Karen State in absence of an independent state. They named their state 'Kawthoolei', meaning 'land of flowers', and to protect it, KNDO continued hostilities as guerrillas, besieging the Burmese as Aung San had foreseen.

'God, protect me,' Lieutenant Maung Kyaw Win prayed under his breath on receiving his orders for the day—escort a train across hostile terrain that night and cross a bridge over a ravine until it reached a beleaguered army garrison situated about 160 kilometres away. The garrison had come under attack a few nights ago, losing a good number of its soldiers to commando style raid by a strong force of the KNDO until they were repelled. The garrison was to be reinforced by 400 soldiers whom the train was carrying that evening and, after fortifying the garrison, the army had decided to conduct a search and destroy the operation, and to put an end to the menace of the guerrillas. 'Everything in order?' asked Lieutenant Maung Kyaw Win.

'Absolutely fine, sir,' replied the driver of the armoured car who was to pilot the train that evening.

'This is a real beauty, Lieutenant. We should have had them earlier, sir. We wouldn't have lost so many trains to those devils.'

'We learn from experience, soldier,' remarked the lieutenant. 'My worry is that those devils will, too.'

'Ah…their bullets can't penetrate this armour, sir,' responded the driver, proudly giving the armoured plate of the vehicle a resounding slap. He felt impervious to harm behind the protective shield of the armoured plates and was grateful to the government for providing the army with these weapons.

'All right,' the lieutenant said, 'let's board now.'

Two soldiers moved into the armoured car along with the driver—one of them seating himself behind the heavy machine gun with its lethal snout pointing out of the turret defiantly, while the other took command of the turret's cannon. Lieutenant Maung Kyaw Win then took overall command of the mechanized monster and waved the engine driver of the train to follow, as an orange sun began to bask on the eastern horizon.

'We will close the hatch in one hour,' the lieutenant announced as the armoured car fired its engines and majestically rolled ahead on its iron wheels.

There was still light in the sky and the lieutenant personally disliked the claustrophobic quarters of the armoured vehicle. He did not share the invulnerability the driver of the vehicle exuded earlier at the station, nor was he inspired by the awesome look of the army's prime weapon. Armour or no armour, the vehicle was a sitting duck for dynamite, and he was hoping that the new phenomenon would temporarily arrest the intrepidity of the insurgents who had become accustomed to blowing up unescorted trains.

'The *Kayin*s (Burmese for Karen) will be surprised,' gleefully commented the machine gunner, eager for an encounter to inaugurate his formidable toy.

'My cannon will blast them to hell, don't forget,' remarked the soldier manning the turret, wishing for the moment when he would display his expertise at gunnery.

'Be alert, comrades. And stop jabbering,' ordered the lieutenant. 'Let's hope that this one gets through. Our fellows at the garrison need us.'

The lieutenant's command silenced the enthusiastic prattle in the armoured car as the steel monster lumbered over the rail track, clacking the distance as it drew closer to the bridge.

*

At the Bridge
An Hour Later

'I can see the headlights,' reported the crouching phantom by the rails on the bridge.

'That's not the train,' observed another. 'I think it's the armoured car our man informed us about.'

'Then it's definitely a military train behind it,' asserted another apparition which arose tall from the chiaroscuro shadows of the descending night and whistled. The shrill, sharp signal stirred a flurry of ghostly silhouettes that glided away from the rails towards the bottom of the ravine.

'We will not engage them in combat this time. They're bound to be a large body,' the tall, commanding silhouette advised when the phantoms had congregated below.

'What do you propose?' asked a shadow.

'Very simple, my dear fellow,' answered the commanding voice. 'I've wired both ends of the bridge. I'll wait until the armoured care reaches the other side and signals the train with an all-clear sign. The train will follow and when most of the coaches are on the bridge, I'll detonate both ends of it and send them plunging to the bottom of the ravine.'

'Fantastic!' exclaimed an insurgent in ecstasy.

'Don't open fire,' warned the commander. 'It is going to betray our position.'

'Okay, boss,' obeyed the shadows around the commander.

'As soon as the dynamites go off, I want everyone to scatter and regroup quietly at the town, understand? Quietly,' he reiterated, and proceeded to take up position for the assault on the bridge.

The armoured car inched cautiously and suspiciously across the bridge—its powerful searchlight turned on and challenging the adversaries of the night with its blinding glare, daring them to a confrontation. Lieutenant Maung Kyaw Win strained his eyes through the slits of the armoured car apprehensively, sweeping the tracks ahead for signs of sabotage. The turret gunner, revolving with the glare of the searchlight, solicited with his alert cannon a target for obliteration; the machine gunner's trigger itched to explode in a soliloquy of death, but to their disappointment, the armoured car railed to the end of the bridge without incident. Deciding that there was no impending attack at least for the night, Lieutenant Maung Kyaw Win, overwhelmed with relief, gave the clear sign to the train—steaming and hissing with anticipation on the other side—to follow.

'Now!' signalled the commander of the phantoms, as a stretch of coaches outlined the length of the bridge. Two pairs of resolute hands firmly pushed down the plungers of the device that sent their charge to the two ends of the bridge. In an instant, the bridge erupted with an infernal roar, tossing the coaches high into the air in a mesh of fiery timber, steel and pulped flesh as the remnants of the train and the bridge tumbled down into the ravine below.

'Retreat, now,' ordered the tall silhouette, leaving an astounded Lieutenant Maung Kyaw Win to witness the raging inferno he had just escaped. And by the time the lieutenant's speechless men regained their soldierly poise behind their monstrous weapons, the silhouettes below the demolished bridge had vanished into the depths of the night.

'I'll get one of those monsters one of these days,' vowed the phantom commander—the last of the silhouettes to merge into the night—watching the brightly lit armoured car against the burning skyline, whirring its turret and seeking out the perpetrators of the catastrophe, before he joined his men with an intoxicating sense of accomplishment.

Judson's Converts

Pyapon
A Karen Township
Southern Burma
Behind the Line of Control
1949–1950

The town was actually an enlarged village that had developed a haphazard infrastructure out of necessity, taking upon itself the need to support a swelling populace descending from the hill tracks near the Thai border; families that had sought to escape from the war of attrition between the insurgents and the government troops. Otherwise its features were typical of Karen village, with bamboo houses elevated on high stilts. The stilts were a geographical and climatic exigency which prevented these houses form being washed away during the torrential monsoon that poured upon the region seasonally. The wealthier of the inhabitants used teak instead of bamboo.

Pigs and buffaloes—the main domesticated livestock of these simple people—milled about the mud, sparking an occasional quarrel when an animal strayed onto a crop of vegetables painstakingly grown by a neighbour. Almost every home boasted of a coop of chickens, a pen of ducks or a gaggle of geese, while the earlier inhabitants owned, in addition, acres of rich paddy land.

The people themselves personified a state of existence which was untouched by the inhabitants and complexities of urban living.

Their festivities were great moments of excitement, pronounced by a sense of joyous abandon when the young and supple would energetically entertain a mesmerized community with native balladry and their spirited traditional dance—rapturously hopping in and out of the clashing bamboo, the movements of their nimble feet dictated by the rhythmic beat of an ancient folklore.

Gloan Na Na Gloan Na na
Too Ley Ley au Ley, Too Ley Ley au Ley Hey
Too Lay Ley au Lay
Too Ley Ley au Ley

These occasions would be heralded with a display of colours, for the entire community would adorn their best, bright and distinctive tribal costumes, differentiating age and gender and bringing out the inherent friendliness and generosity of the people. Every home would have a ready menu of the choicest food, and would not let a visitor depart without relishing the exquisiteness of its hospitality.

These quaint people could have easily been taken for pagans or animists until one saw the big gathering at an unostentatious church on the hill on a Sunday morning—all singing with their lovely voices, with touching choirs and solemn hymns, praying to God and Jesus Christ with fervour for deliverance from their sins and protection from an occasional wayward Burmese soldier. Generations ago, an evangelical Adoniram Judson and his fellow missionary George Broadman, spreading the Gospel along the pagan hill tracks of Burma and unmindful of the perils of death and disease, had reached these white Karens and converted the majority of them to Christianity. In 1828, Judson found in Ko Tha Byu, a fierce guerrilla fighting the Burmese, their first Karen apostle. Tha Byu spread the message of Christianity, and since then, those converted have remained staunch Baptists.

But much before the Bible reached them, the Karens talk of a golden book which depicts the creation of man—stunningly, an echo of the Old Testament's *Genesis*!

The book, according to them, said that Father God created heaven and earth and having created heaven and earth, He created the sun, the moon and the stars. Having created the sun, the moon and the stars, He created man from the earth. Having created man, He created woman from a rib out of the man. Having created woman, He created life. Having created life, Father God said, 'I love my son and daughter; I will give them my great life', and took a little portion of his own life, breathed into the nostrils of the two persons and they came to life, and were real human beings. He then created food and drink. He created rice, He created water, He created fire, He created cows, He created elephants and He created birds.

Having created animals, Father God said, 'My son and daughter, your father will make and give you a garden. In the garden are seven different kinds of trees, bearing seven different kinds of fruits. Among the seven, one tree is not good to eat from. Do not eat of its fruit. If you eat it, you will become old, you will die. Eat it not. All else that I have created, I give to you. Eat and drink to the full. Once in seven days, I will visit you. All that I have commanded, you observe and do. Forget me not. Pray to me every morning and night.' The Karens made sure that they never missed on Sundays.

Life was good to him, thought U Saw Too fleetingly on one such Sunday morning. He was an elder and respected widely by the townsfolk. His family had plenty to eat and clothe themselves. They lived in a large house, the only one built with brick and mortar—considered an edifice of wealth in the community. Complying with the Japanese occupation forces for supply of food and route directions, and the British for intelligence gathering on their return to Burma, his family had survived the Japanese occupation, the allied bombing and the repercussions of the abortive insurrection. All seemed well with U Saw Too's family for the present, except that Dora wasn't satisfied.

Dora was his fourth child and had, since her young years, displayed a precociousness which had surprised him, for he hadn't expected it in a daughter. She saw no future in the town and was disenchanted with the prospect of settling down with a townsman and perpetuating a life of tediousness, nor was she enamoured with the prospect of being widowed by a local hero. Like a few of her generation, Dora had yearned to seek emancipation from the confines of provincial life, and longed instead for brave new horizons in the quest for self-discovery. She had done well at school and was equally successful at the secretarial institute, and was ready to test her mettle in a large city environment. She was confident of doing well in Rangoon.

U Saw Too had his own apprehensions about the future of the town, although he seldom spoke about them. The town, he knew, had a commercial significance for the KNDO; like many other towns, it was not free of its filial ties with the KNDO. Apart from the purchase of goods and medical supplies, the KNDO had occasionally fallen back upon it, seeking temporary sanctuary after a raid across the line of control. What saddened U Saw Too was that, whether it was a question of political obligation or moral rectitude, there wasn't a way of stopping this dangerous traffic; the prevention of commerce or the hiding of a fugitive.

It would only be a matter of time before this placid little town lost its beatitude, he sighed with regret. There was already a murmur spreading among the youth, their imagination inflamed by the exploits of some leaders against the Burmese. Audacious and unorthodox, these leaders were creating a legend of their own and becoming venerated by a cult-prone youth, feared U Saw Too, but what alarmed him was the nature of some of these exploits.

The insurrection was a wound yet to heal in the national memory, and in the absence of a truce or negotiation, military skirmishes were to be expected in the defence of one's ideals and principles. But penetrating into the army camps deep in Burmese territory and massacring soldiers was outrageous, felt U Saw Too, with disdain. He was further appalled at the news of rail bridges being blown up along with the trains, including non-military ones, inflicting death and injury upon innocent civilians.

All these were inexcusable provocations that would only tarnish their cause and strengthen the government's resolve to avoid dialogue, U Saw Too thought wearily. He was, therefore, not surprised at the reprisal of the soldiers—deplorable as they were—whenever they chanced upon an unsuspecting Karen village across the line of control; plundering, burning and killing some of the luckless villagers who hadn't escaped. It was a small price the Karen people were paying for the adventures of a few foolish men, he thought, but for how long the price would remain small, he wondered.

The government was predominantly Buddhist and pacifist, the army still adolescent and weak at the moment, mostly engaged in police action in a country that was going through the throes of political evolution, but U Saw Too's wisdom warned him that the situation could change and when it did, he had no doubt that the Burmese would exact a stiffer price from his people.

As U Saw Too was engrossed with his concerns of the future for the Karens, he noticed a fellow elder who was a covert visitor from Kawthoolei on a regular intelligence-gathering mission. The elder passed him and whispered, 'Sea Prince has blown up a bridge again, I heard.' After a pregnant pause, 'Full of soldiers...full of soldiers,' said the man, his eyes aglow with awe.

'What! Sea Prince?' stuttered U Saw Too in disbelief. 'Again?'

'Yes, Brother Saw Too,' replied the elder, 'last night.'

'But the papers said that he was shot dead by the soldiers last month!'

'The papers tell you mostly what the government tells them, Brother Saw Too,' replied the fellow elder. 'The man is indestructible.'

'Yes, yes, I suppose so,' U Saw Too replied hesitantly.

The papers had reported, recollected U Saw Too, the death of Sea Prince several times, but each time a report came, the elusive Sea Prince would arise from the ashes like a phoenix and blow up another bridge—waiting until the next report when he would blow up yet another bridge. Sea Prince was a self-styled commander who assumed fancy names and preposterous ranks that usually hovered between brigadier and general. He went by the title of *Tharah*, which was an equivalent of the English 'Master'. And now he's blown up another bridge, U Saw Too learned from his fellow elder.

'Did you say a military train?' asked U Saw Too, suspecting the contrary. 'Where were the soldiers going?'

'They are after Alexander. You must have heard of his attack on the Burmese garrison.'

'Ah! You could be right,' U Saw Too remarked. He had heard about the attack as well, and shuddered at the mention of Alexander's name.

A contemporary of Sea Prince, Alexander was another growing legend of a ubiquitous Karen general who was a master military tactician. His specialty was attacking garrisons of the Burmese Army. Ruthless and uncompromising in his beliefs, the Burmese Army had, on every confrontation, suffered staggering losses at his hands. While Sea Prince remained enigmatic and surreptitious with his escapades, this general had the habit of firmly imprinting his signature on his exploits, and was famed for forewarning the enemy of his impending attack. He was known to never have taken prisoners, and was feared by the Burmese. This Karen general, flushed with incredible success, even had the audacity to sneak into Rangoon to visit a mistress. The Karens themselves rarely contradicted him, for there were none amongst them who had the temerity to tame the violence in this general.

'I hope there weren't any civilians on the train,' said U Saw Too.

'What difference does that make?' countered his fellow elder. 'It's the civilians who are sending these troops, aren't they? The Burmese have to realize that they can never dominate us and the sooner they give us what we want, the sooner we will leave them and their bridges alone.'

'Brother, don't you see that all this will only hurt us and undermine our cause?' implored U Saw Too. 'The Burmese papers will only write stories of Karen atrocities and the world is going to believe them.'

'We aren't worried about the world or what it thinks,' snapped the elder. 'Look at what that Indian did! Sent a shipload of arms just when we were about to capture Rangoon.'

'That's exactly what I'm talking about—international opinion,' argued U Saw Too. 'We aren't legitimate in the eyes of the world yet, and the only way we can achieve it is by negotiation. Even the British left us stranded.'

'Yes, you see? It's exactly what I mean. The world is not going to help us, and it's up to us now to find a place under the sun for ourselves, our wives and our children. We have no other way,' the elder insisted.

'The government will send more and more soldiers until there will not be a Karen left to go to the negotiating table,' retorted U Saw Too.

'Ha!' scoffed the elder. 'Let them just try. As long as we have the likes of Sea Prince and General Alexander, no soldier of the Burmese Army will dare come near us. There won't be a bridge left even if they wanted to.'

U Saw Too recoiled at the elder's remark and wisely decided to refrain from further talk. He had no desire to provoke the elder into denouncing him as a traitor to the KNDO, who were a bunch of ill-disciplined hot heads as far as he was concerned, and was certain that the lack of discipline in the ranks had been the chief cause of the failure of the insurrection. The Indian shipload of arms was still a week away when they began losing their grip on the initiative. The KNDO didn't seem to have a major or a colonel, let alone lieutenant and captain in their clandestine army—they were all generals, U Saw Too thought sarcastically, and didn't know whether to laugh or to be angry when he suddenly felt a great anxiety from the ignorant youth who would spill their blood, extolling these legends. He grieved for a generation of maidens who would never attain motherhood.

'The Burmese don't understand the meaning of negotiation. They understand force, Brother Saw Too,' the elder nodded his grey grim head in finality. 'Just pray that we don't run out of heroes like Sea Prince and Alexander.'

'Yes…yes, of course,' hastened U Saw Too in reply, concealing his personal misgivings.

These were the kind of legends that U Saw Too feared most, the kind of legend that had a double edge—one, of a criminal, and the other, a hero; a kind of legend the youth worshipped and a kind of legend that would pervert the original perspective of the cause of nationhood for a people.

Even some right-thinking elders had succumbed to these legends, confirming sadly to U Saw Too the need of a people for their heroes. All these thoughts were storming his mind when he remembered that he had to take Dora to Rangoon the next day. The girl had been difficult and wouldn't be persuaded otherwise. She wanted to leave the town at the earliest opportunity, and stay with a relative's family in the city until she secured suitable employment.

U Saw Too was perplexed at the changing values of this generation. Imagine! She, his daughter! Daring to go to Rangoon? And demanding from him her freedom? On the other hand, he thought in resignation, it must be God's will for the better. After a pause, he foreboded that the town would hold no future for many of his people.

I will take the river to Rangoon, he decided, at last wanting to avoid the train.

U Saw Too wasn't very comfortable with the thought and the image of *Tharah* Sea Prince or his lurking ghost stalking a bridge in the dark.

*

The Irrawaddy River

The waters were of an old river. The Irrawaddy had its tertiary origins in the Himalayan heights. And in later times, when its upper waters were no longer fed by the Tibetan Tsan-Po and in angry demonstration of geographical will, it gathered its momentum from the Chindwin and its twin. Altering character at its confluence and rebelliously coursing through a changing topography in its strife to attain an independent identity, the brownish-yellow surge rushed along with strong currents, carrying away in its torrent debris and refuse of man and nature. And as it neared Rangoon, the river, now burdened with the constantly shifting silt and slush, revolted again and burst into several fractious estuaries, each choosing to travel a different path to self-realization, and its ultimate integration with the Timeless One—the Indian Ocean.

It was symbolic of the torment of a nation grappling with its karma for its ultimate attainment of nirvana. The river had seen the tumult of time devastate this land and, in ancient times, had attested to the birth and purge of local kingdoms, the invasion of foreigners and its own aggression of a southern neighbour. It had seen its great King Anaurata embrace Buddhism, and abolish an evil practice prevalent in the kingdom. Known then as 'Pun-Ooh Hlu', the ritual called for the first seeding of the bride by this ecclesiastic segment of their society, whereby the priests had first claim to the nuptials in the land.

It saw Thee Baw, the last king the country was to have, and his vicious queen named Suphahla, whose sadistic delight was in having those who fell from her grace buried alive while she watched elephants walk over the soft mound of earth, crushing the bones of her hapless victims, spirited away on a British ship to an Indian coast where they would be imprisoned for life.

From the boat, Dora could see the magnificent Shwedagon pagoda towering from the river bank with its beckoning golden glitter under the sun, silently promising, as it had in the past, the peace and culture of ahimsa amongst the people of the land, and hoped that her decision to come to Rangoon was indeed the right one.

'Thank you, Father,' she said as father and daughter got off the boat, making their way to the city.

U Saw Too remained silent and wondered how many of his family would soon follow Dora, with the hope of escaping the mundane and make a living in Rangoon. He might consider moving to Rangoon himself if things were good enough, he thought, but that had to wait a while, for there were things in town to attend to.

He left his daughter in the care of his relatives, providing her with some money, and took the boat back to Pyapon.

Dora was now in Rangoon, a wish fulfilled. And in a few days' time, she occupied herself with the task of self-support and independence. Rangoon was a city rebuilding itself. Japanese war reparation and Allied compensation were pouring into the country, and the city was fast resuming its commercial significance in South East Asia. With its developing port, shipping increased; with shipping flourished numerous shipping companies. Indians, Singaporeans and Hong Kong-Chinese, and even the Japanese, poured in to forge profitable partnerships in a country that was experiencing a prospering post-war economy.

Managerial and administrative, clerical and secretarial staff, and all kinds of employment opportunities became available to those found enterprising and competent enough to shoulder the responsibility of running these businesses. Dora found no difficulty in obtaining a niche for herself in this post-war prosperity of the capital, and was soon sitting in the office of a Japanese shipping company, awaiting her interview for a secretarial position in the company.

'Send her in,' sounded a deep baritone that was authoritative but pleasant. Dora had never been more surprised in her life until she met face-to-face with the source of the impressive voice. He was an Indian!

Stanley sat behind the desk and looked at the applicant, assessing the candidate for potential in the demanding and overworked environment of shipping. It didn't occur to him then that his Asian dream that had eluded him all along was to culminate with the interview.

The General

Rangoon, 1962

The death of Aung San had receded in the national consciousness as a memory to be rekindled once a year with solemnity. A statue was erected to be adulated by the people while framed photographs adorned government offices and private dwellings, but beyond the frame of the photographs and the ornamentation, the benign smile of Aung San had lost its charisma over the political process of the country.

Rivalry and corruption amidst Buddhist piety was taking its toll on the government, turning it unstable and weaker by the month; the avaricious manipulated the circumstances to their benefit, spreading an atmosphere of disillusionment among the educated and the common folk.

They were now looking for a change.

They desired a strong government that could control the soaring prices in the marketplace and contain the insurgencies that made living and travelling in the far regions mortally dangerous. The army had to lead the trains with armoured cars, which didn't deter the insurgents who blew them up along with the trains, and the bridges.

The people wanted peace in the land and a rightful opportunity for prosperity, which was now held mostly in foreign hands. And in some quarters, they wanted the erosion of Buddhist values to stop. The land had its share of gallivanting amorous monks who hadn't entirely forsaken the way of the flesh.

But they did not have an answer to an alternative. They didn't trust the communists, nor did they have faith in the many parties that promised political reform. They had only U Nu—a devout Buddhist—a factor they had no problem with, except that he was not delivering. The years had dragged on until their deliverance came, and it came in the uniform of a general.

Ne Win!

Now a general, Ne Win had, on a previous occasion, briefly taken control of the country's affairs under the initiation of U Nu. After sorting out the political chaos, he had then returned the country to civilian rule. General Ne Win was again ready to give the country the change it wanted, and took the initiative without an invitation from the government of U Nu.

This time, the general staged the coup!

The general's sudden swoop and deposition of U Nu's government was widely hailed by the people as a refreshing prelude to a stable civilian government in the near future, just as he had done in the past for them. Foreigners and citizens alike were jubilant that their way of life could continue—the accumulation of wealth unhindered under the protection of a forceful presence of law, while the local citizenry looked forward to the percolation of prosperity.

The people had no inkling at the time of the general's real intentions of creating a republic—a republic quite different from the one their imagination could have conceived. This time, the general was keeping the country for himself. The general and his junta would reveal their intentions to the unsuspecting public in the ensuing days, taking them to a new vista of fear and suppression.

*

Rangoon, 1962–1966

'Dora,' exclaimed Stanley, 'there's beef in the market. It's amazing!'

It was Stanley's habit to visit the market on certain days when returning home from work and, on that day, he brought a quantity of the meat home.

Known as the dark meat, the Buddhist shied away from it and it was banned during U Nu's rule. Soon after the general and his junta legitimized their government, it became available in the open market. Stanley was surprised at the unique phenomenon. In a land where the cow was venerated as a sacred animal and in deference to the prevalent Buddhist sentiment, the meat was never sold in the markets. And those who ate the meat seldom had an opportunity to procure it.

Strangely, the presence of raw beef fresh from the slaughter had not provoked any noticeable outrage from the public. The meat sold! That was the first visible change Stanley and the rest of the country were to see.

'And it's cheap,' said a visibly excited and happy Stanley, for he could now supplement the nourishment of a growing family with inexpensive nutrition.

'Ne Win is turning this country around,' Stanley said, with admiration for the general. The general, he thought, was pulling the country out from the dark ages of superstition and religious zealotry, and making a modern state of it.

Then, very shortly, Stanley was to notice the unprecedented raise in the standard of living of the army. Young army officers were driving Japanese cars—quite likely part of the war reparation from Japan, while most senior officers in larger neighbouring armies pedalled on bicycles. It was evident to Stanley that it did well for their morale and certainly assured their loyalty. It seemed natural enough that many a young man joined Ne Win's army for the status and the glamour.

Next, on a quiet morning, the streets of Rangoon bore witness to an unaccountably large number of soldiers boarding army trucks, and were converging onto predetermined positions. Most residents presumed that it was preparation for a military parade and gave no further thought to the matter as they went about that morning attending to their business.

*

47th Street
Rangoon
7:30 AM

It was Jimmy's street.

Jimmy felt supreme that morning when he woke up. He stretched his body and vigorously shook the traces of languor that had crept over him during the night in anticipation of the new day's chores to earn a living. He would strut on the street again and entertain passers-by with his usual bag of tricks, unlike most of his mates who preferred to scavenge and laze about during the day.

Just then, his keen ears picked up the distant steps of ammunition boots crunching steadily towards him. Jimmy's instincts warned him that something was afoot in the vicinity. It had been years since he had seen so many soldiers on his street, and experience helped him distinguish between soldiers on furlough and soldiers ready for an act of war. His instincts urged him to flee from the approaching soldiers, but his curiosity betrayed his better judgment, for he had fond memories of soldiers.

They had always fed him.

Jimmy could not believe his eyes when he saw a soldier levelling his rifle at him. 'No! Don't shoot!' Jimmy winced and whined, but felt a searing pain surging through his body when suddenly, without warning, the indolent neighbourhood exploded into gunfire. It caught Jimmy by complete surprise—the image of the soldier who shot him receding in his clouding canine eyes as life seeped out of him.

'They're shooting!' screamed the unnerved residents. The sharp report of the guns raked them with terror and confusion, for they couldn't fathom the reason for the gunfire. While most recoiled to the safe interiors of their windows, a few curious ones peeped out of their windows, trying to comprehend the commotion outside.

'The dogs! They're shooting the dogs....Oh my God!' exclaimed Stanley. Rangoon, at the time, was swarming with dogs—pariahs, mongrels and some with nobler antecedents like Jimmy; pets or mascots—it was anyone's guess but the canine population had mostly been left by their masters from the evacuating army to breed unrestrainedly on the streets of Rangoon. Ne Win's soldiers were shooting stray dogs on sight. Then military trucks rolled down the streets, dispensing poisoned bones for the ones that had managed to dodge the bullets. The poisoned dead would be collected the next day.

Rangoon was being rid of the dogs and would be a cleaner city, Stanley grudgingly acknowledged, but he sensed that the subtlety of the general's exercise was as loud as the gunfire. It was the general's brilliant psychological manoeuvre to acquaint the public with his army. It was time, thought the general, that the people understood him as a decisive man; to understand well that he was not a man with the qualities of a monk, like U Nu, who would be squeamish to find a solution to a vulgar epidemic that plagued his capital. He was a military man and his army was a shooting army. The shooting of the dogs was his subliminal message to the people, but the people soon recovered from their shock and returned to their routine and preoccupation with daily living, feeling sorry for Jimmy and the children who would miss Jimmy's bag of tricks. They had, however, overlooked the significance of the general's message.

*

Scot's Market, Rangoon
11:00 AM

Scot's Market was a modern and fashionable shopping arcade in Rangoon, patronized by the wealthy and the well-to-do among the citizenry of the city where the best of the branded commodities could be purchased. But the atmosphere of affluence that exuded from the commercial complex also attracted its share of mendicancy in the city that preyed upon the Buddhist disposition towards compassion and the general sympathy of the shoppers. Worse still were the lepers who, unfortunate as their circumstance was, aggressively exploited the ugliness and repulsiveness of their aliment to the terror and revulsion of the shoppers.

'Alms! Alms!' shouted Tin Win one such morning, boldly approaching a group of well-dressed shoppers escorted by Stanley, confident that they would voluntarily part with a few kyats to get rid of him as quickly as possible. Tin Win was a leper who thrived unabashedly on the squeamish gentry who thought money was the only ablution they had in distancing themselves from the horror of his disease. It suited Tin Win if they absolved themselves of the blame by their token of charity, for their weakness was the guarantee of his profession.

'Here, take this and be gone,' Stanley said, dropping a few kyats into the outstretched bowl in the ulcerated hand of Tin Win.

'*Cheyzu tin ba dae, saya gee* (thank you, Big Master),' Tin Win responded with the grin of a winner. He was never wrong with his judgement of human weakness or character. 'May God bless you with many children and may you have a place for your family in heaven.'

'Damned nuisance,' muttered Stanley, not flattered or moved by the beggar's expression of gratitude. He had just been called *saya gee* (Big Master), and Stanley wondered whether the beggar suspected that he already had a swollen family.

'It's quite a menace, isn't it?' remarked one of Stanley's guests as he shepherded the group of visitors from the head office on a tour of the country away from the accosting Tin Win.

'Shouldn't the government be doing something about it?' asked another.

The government was indeed planning on a course of action. Warnings had been issued to the lepers in particular to report to the centre for internment, but Tin Win and his associates had been obstinate. It was this morning that the government decided to make good the warning. To the utter surprise of Stanley and his group of visitors, military trucks appeared suddenly from nowhere, unloading armed soldiers who surrounded the market and cordoned off the area. A detachment of soldiers with rifles unslung, and led by a grim-looking officer, marched into the complex—creating a stir among the shoppers and shopkeepers alike.

'Run! The soldiers are coming,' Tin Win frantically hollered at his leprous mates.

'*Payaa! Payaa* (God! God!)!' screamed the lepers in fright.

What followed next was a sight, both comical and pathetic, that Stanley would long remember. The lepers were running helter-skelter, shouting and cursing—some collapsing on their crutches and crying out to God, beseeching divine intervention. Some tucked in their longyis to enhance their mobility, discovering in their fright a strength within hidden by years of beggary as they bounded—their begging bowls askew, spilling their morning's rake in their flight straight into the net of the soldiers waiting outside the market.

With no avenue for escape, the lepers were prodded by the rifles of the soldiers and herded towards a large van parked alongside the military trucks. The immunity of the untouchable that Tin Win and the likes of him shielded themselves with was inadequate armour in the presence of the cold steel of the guns pointing at them. Meekly, they boarded the van and as the van began to pull out from Scot's Market, Tin Win—now deprived of his immunity—looked at the complex forlornly with a premonition that he would never enjoy his reign of terror again, nor would he live to nurture its memory.

Stanley heard a hushed rumour a few days later that the lepers had been administered with poison injections, and later cremated en masse. He wasn't sure of the veracity of the whisper but he did notice that the lepers had disappeared, and with them, the beggary that had thrived on Buddhist benevolence had disappeared, too.

The cleansing of Rangoon had begun in earnest.

By this time, unease had set in amongst the people. The people, predominantly Buddhists, were shocked. Their sense of piety found the extremity of the army revolting, while for the others, it was the beginning of fear and insight. This was not a foreign army that was flouting the tenets of Buddhism but their own, and it had shown its abject disregard for life—or for that matter, the serious issue of reincarnation and the laws of cause and effect.

*

The Campus
Rangoon University
July 1962

The university was founded in 1878. The campus looked relatively new, exuding a vibrant aura of fresh scholarship and erudition; its lawn green with regularly mowed grass and evenly spaced trees, radiant with their spring bloom. The campus had endeavoured to produce a generation of alumni like U Thant, the first UN secretary general, Aung San, U Nu and General Ne Win. Many lead illustrious lives in various capacities in the country and abroad, while it had hoped to retain some from the younger generation who would choose to remain and bolster the portals of enlightenment.

Maung Baa Kyi was a final-year student on the campus, majoring in political science. Though he was an erudite student, and his professors and lecturers initially took great pleasure in tutoring him, they would soon discover that he was not the protégé they had expected. Maung Baa Kyi was a popular breeze that was blowing through the campus, frowned upon by the conventional among the teachers as a contagion and a threat to the sacred portals of their cherished institution, while most others were stimulated with curiosity and warmth by his outspokenness and fearlessness.

Maung Baa Kyi was not certain that the policies of the military government augured well for the country. He had sensed a tightening of the military fist around the free spirit of learning and enquiry in the country, and had debated with his fellow scholars and peers the issue of rights in a democracy. He had argued vehemently with visiting military officials to the faculty the difference between a rightfully elected government and the imposition of a military dictatorship upon a nation, depriving it of a voice in the rule of its people.

Maung Baa Kyi was a patriot at heart in the tradition of Aung San, and his intellect was outraged by the strangulation of his nation by a totalitarianism that was not intrinsically Burmese but Russian or Chinese. He began to organize innocuous meetings—initially on the campus—putting forth his views, but they soon caught the attention of a larger number of students and some of the teaching staff. The meetings gradually grew in number until they could no longer be kept a secret. And within no time, his activity blossomed into a movement, much to the concern of the heads of the university. They now feared a movement that would take the university to the precipice of a major tragedy unless they acted fast. They had to ban Maung Baa Kyi's student union.

'Hey, Baa Kyi,' called out a classmate as he entered the campus one morning. 'The professor wants to see you urgently.'

'Yeah? What about?' parried Maung Baa Kyi. 'I have to attend a meeting now.'

'It's about the meeting he wants to see you.'

'Oh. What's up?' Maung Baa Kyi asked, but was unable to elicit an answer as the student had wriggled into the crowd of aspiring undergraduates.

'Hey, wait!' he called out and realized that his classmate had vanished. There were only the few curious faces staring at him and distancing him as a rebel.

'What are you looking at, you imbeciles!' he yelled at them and stormed into the professors' chamber.

'So, Professor San Yu, I have been told that you wanted to see me regarding my meeting,' confronted Maung Baa Kyi, ignoring the conventional code of bowing in Burmese society that elders expected of their youngsters.

'Oh! Baa Kyi, come…come. Take a seat please,' Professor San Yu greeted his student and sighed heavily, having noticed the agitation in the student's voice.

'Yes, Baa Kyi,' replied Professor San Yu. 'Your meetings will have to stop. I've just received orders from the vice-chancellor.' Professor San Yu met the confrontation head-on, intuiting that it was the best way to defuse the simmering tension in his student.

'Why, professor? This is a centre of learning and education. How can I, as an educated person, stop these meetings? We all know that very soon this country will be another country like the Soviet Union or China. And the people have a right to know that.'

'Baa Kyi, please listen to me,' entreated Professor San Yu. 'I can understand your concerns and the fire in you, but do remember that you are still a student and not a politician, and you owe it to me as my best student to heed the voice of common sense and caution.'

'I have a great regard for you, sir. And that won't change, whatever may happen. But the fact is that our generation, apparently, is the only one left with a voice,' Maung Baa Kyi retorted. 'I can't imagine how this generation will take up responsibilities of building the nation in the near future if we can't be allowed to reason and exercise our minds. Or is it that this education is about how to be mindless mutes?'

Professor San Yu reddened at Maung Baa Kyi's rhetoric. It pained him that his brightest student had questioned the purpose of the haloed portals of the institution, and the challenge annoyed him ever more, for he did not have an answer as to how one could alienate expression from an intellectual process.

'Are you sure you are voicing your intellect or are you just being a pawn of some scheming ex-politician? I know you have been hobnobbing with a few of them of late,' Professor San Yu shot back, the rebuttal silencing Maung Baa Kyi for a moment.

'Professor, please believe me. I speak from the depth of my conscience only,' he answered. 'Unless we voice our thoughts loudly and demonstrate our conviction, this country will remain in the hands of military dictators for all our lives.'

'Baa Kyi, I share your view and I'm proud that a student of mine has the courage to live up to his convictions, but please do not continue with these meetings on this campus. Take them elsewhere. And for you own sake, I hope you know what you are up against,' said Professor San Yu, hoping that his student could take a hint.

Maung Baa Kyi rose from his chair and left the professors' chamber without further comment, and walked towards his appointment. He felt guilty that he was betraying a greater trust placed on him by his professor. The Rangoon University was no exception in that like most universities, it was a hotbed for political activists, budding revolutionaries and reformers who would question authority. It did just that on that fateful morning. The students, led by a determined Maung Baa Kyi, staged a vociferous and reckless agitation in the campus, demanding a return to democracy.

*

'Dora,' an unnerved Stanley said when he returned home that evening, 'a terrible thing has happened today. I can't believe this is happening in the country, but we'll read about it in the papers tomorrow morning, I'm sure.'

Stanley's disposition provoked instant alarm in Dora.

'What are you talking about?' she asked. He then told her the sordid story.

'My God!' she exclaimed. 'This is horrible news.'

'Yes. It's very sad,' Stanley replied, shaking his head sadly.

'What will they do next?' he asked himself woefully, and remembered what Murray had told him.

Most people knew that university students had been fomenting a confrontation with the army for over a week. They were denouncing the military government of General Ne Win. Stanley learnt that morning that the military had swung in instantaneously and surrounded the university campus. Insanely, the few warnings given were ignored by the riotous students who, incensed by the presence of the military, flung back insults at the guns pointing at them. The guns were not just meant to scare them. The general had said, 'Guns are not meant for pointing upwards!' The soldiers needed no further instigation. They opened fire, mowing down the students and snuffing out the voices that had dared to cry out for democracy. Maung Baa Kyi fell with the first volley, his fragile body broken by six bullets. His body was not released to his parents but was buried in an unmarked grave, his dreams to die with him in anonymity. The army had shot to kill that day. And to further ensure the omnipotence of the regime, army engineers blew up a section of the university building where the student union was located, where they suspected the remnants of the rabble was hiding.

That day, in the year 1962, was another dark day in the modern history of the country since the assassination of Aung San, a bewildering day that astounded and traumatized parents and citizens—a violent day that finally awoke the people from any delusion of their new reality. The army was now shooting human beings; their children and future citizens of the country. It was not a benevolent general who sat at the helm of the nation's affairs, but a belligerent dictator who was insensitive to any language other than the one spoken in the dialect of the gun.

*

Satisfied with the effect he had achieved, the general and his junta then embarked upon an economic policy that was to have severe consequences for the country, its people and the foreigners who had elected to settle down in Burma. The general announced to the country that he was introducing economic reforms for the betterment of the country. The national economic programme espoused by the regime as 'The Burmese Way to Socialism' was ostensibly to distribute the wealth of the nation amongst its citizens. In reality, it meant dispossessing foreigners of their property and businesses with immediate effect.

'The Burmese Way to Confiscation' saw former landlords and proprietors of businesses subdued and humbled for a change on the streets of Rangoon, which most thought was justifiable punishment. Landlords and moneylenders who were unmerciful with their victims were discreetly begging and borrowing now.

'Damned good! The fellows deserve it, Murray,' remarked Stanley while discussing the subject with his neighbour one evening, returning from work.

'Mostly your chaps, Stanley,' said Murray with a grin.

'It would appear so, Murray,' conceded Stanley. 'But I'm sure the Indians are not the only ones; they have their own, you know.'

The lieutenant who had taken in Stanley and his men during the war as prisoners had remained in post-war Burma like some of his countrymen, and had settled down, marrying a Burmese lady and spawning the last generation of Anglo-Burmese. Murray now worked as a journalist for a local English newspaper called *The Burma Star*.

'It's a good thing that you're not a businessman now,' commented Murray. 'The loss would have been more mournful.'

'Quite right, Murray,' replied Stanley grudgingly, recollecting that the total personal wealth he could have ever claimed as his own had become ashes in his memory now.

But Stanley was indebted to the lieutenant, for it was him who had helped Stanley set up a canteen for the soldiers until the evacuation with the approval of Colonel MacIntyre, retired since in the United Kingdom. The great irony of his life, Stanley reflected. It was the British who imprisoned him, and then helped him after the war to start a business; and when the business had suffered a disaster, it was the Japanese again who had given him a job until he found better opportunities with an American company, for which he was now working.

'It was bound to happen,' Murray commented.

'What?' asked Stanley, recovering from the wistful knowledge that fate had denied him success in becoming the prosperous businessman that he had wanted to be.

'The disparity in wealth is too visible,' Murray said.

'Oh that! Yes, Murray. Most of the country's commerce is either in the hands of the Chinese or our chaps,' agreed Stanley.

'Yes,' observed Murray. 'Few Burmese have any say in the economy of the country.'

'I realized that and I do sympathize with them,' Stanley said.

'But not any more from what I see,' said Murray. 'It appears to me that the Burmese are going to have the only say now.'

'Oh! The general's doing okay, Murray,' Stanley responded. 'It's only natural that he restores a balance of some sort.'

Stanley himself had detested the greed of his countrymen who had little regard for the honour of the Burmese, and he saw the general's policies as a natural consequence. He had no sympathy for the moneylenders, the land-grabbers and the building owners, whether they were countrymen of his or not. There had to be the question of honour and fairness in life which he cherished, and he was not about to surrender his beliefs despite the looming threat of his own survival in the political atmosphere that was getting more and more unpredictable.

'I'm afraid I won't be here long enough to find out,' informed Murray. 'The family and I have decided to move far away, to Australia, in a month's time.'

'Why not the UK?' enquired Stanley.

'I believe I'll have better opportunities in Australia, Stanley,' replied Murray. 'Britain's pretty beat up at the moment, you know; what with practically giving away the empire and all that!'

'Ha! Ha!' laughed Stanley at Murray's wisecrack.

The war had left them with a sense of humour and they enjoyed sharing it between them. It also reflected the strength of their relationship.

'Oh no, Murray, what about the wealth of the colonies you chaps have drained from them?' Stanley rebutted.

'Ha! Ha!' It was Murray's turn to laugh. 'You don't expect to get the railways, the telegraph, the postal services and a whole administrative service for free, do you now?'

'And I suppose you'd say we got it cheap?' chided Stanley in rebuff.

'Yes, believe me, Stanley,' Murray said, seemingly serious. 'Yes, you have, unless you folks want to carry on with bullock carts. We'd charge you the sky for every motor car or locomotive you import from us, you know.'

'Very imperialistic, isn't it? Or is it capitalism? Anyway, quite soon you are going to see a whole lot of us in Britain, returning the favour,' Stanley said.

'It's strange, isn't it? We give you the independence to leave you alone so that you can enjoy it, and what do you do? You land in England and take away our jobs, not allowing us to enjoy our memories of having been your masters,' Murray remarked with a wide grin.

'That's the way of the world,' answered Stanley. 'It's karmic, you know.'

'Ah! You keep saying that. Karma! I'm inclined to believe in the here and now…in what you sow and reap in one lifetime. Not in something a few births away which I won't recognize. Anyway, what about you, Stanley?' asked Murray, returning to the topic of the general's junta. 'Plan to stay on here?'

'Yes,' replied Stanley confidently. 'I'm sure things will level down once the general's through with the balancing act.'

'In that case, you'd better do something about your citizenship,' advised Murray. 'I don't think it's going to stop here. There's an ill wind blowing, as the saying goes, but take it from me as a newspaper man, it'll get worse.'

'Oh, it won't be that bad, Murray,' Stanley answered. 'It's principally just the matter of trade and labour that has to be resolved and after that, I'm sure things will be just fine. I'm married to a national after all.'

'Sure. But she's a Karen. You would be quite stupid to ignore it,' cautioned Murray.

Stanley was certain that once the economic balance was restored in the country, life would return to normalcy again. He was wrong. In the following months, he was to see how wrong he was, and began to feel disturbed by the zealous extent to which the general's policies were implemented.

*

THE ECONOMIC REVOLUTION

Kamayut
A Suburb of Rangoon
8:00 AM

Mohamed Ibrahim was a second-generation Indian in Burma. Belonging to a community called the Kha Khas, his ancestors came from a southern state in India commonly known as Malabar. Surprisingly for a Kha Kha, he spoke Burmese fluently and, but for his skin, was as Burmese as the locals. He went to a local school with the Burmese and wore his lungi as the Burmese did. He read the news in Burmese and wrote his accounts in Burmese. His nativity in India was as remote to him now as it was to many of his kind who had settled in the country and practiced a business in which the community excelled. They ran utility and provision stores all around Rangoon and its suburbs, and provided a service that the native Burmese were yet to perfect. Credit without interest.

The store he owned was his pride and, like his father who had started the business, he was known to be fair in his dealings. His dream was to find someone capable of looking after the business, which would allow him an opportunity for a holiday and passage to India, where he would seek a wife and bring her back with him to this land of abundance. Little did he suspect that morning when he woke up that his dreams would end prematurely, and that in a few months' time he would be on-board a refugee ship on a one-way journey to his ancestral home.

That morning, Mohamed Ibrahim saw his provision store sealed and numerically marked. It had a new board in place of the old one, and was now identified as 'People's Stores No. 178'. He panicked and couldn't understand what had happened. He had heard a rumour that the government had plans to abolish private enterprise in the land, and he had presumed it meant the big private sector. His was a small business; far too small for the government to take an interest in. He went about the neighbourhood to determine the facts.

To his horror, he saw that smaller endeavours than his had suffered the same fate. The corner sugarcane juice shop, the tea shop, the barber, the bakery and the small kiosks that dished out snacks to schoolchildren were all now out of business. In a state of destitution now, Mohamed Ibrahim could determine only one common factor that linked his business with all those in the neighbourhood that had ceased to exist. They were all owned by Indians. These petty businessmen who represented the commerce of the country at the bottom level had lost the only asset they had in their lives without recourse to any compensation from the government. Nor did their debtors deem it appropriate to alleviate their state of indigence by honouring the credit given to them.

*

Guhan Singh & Company
Rangoon
9:00 AM

Guhan Singh & Company was a large private enterprise that catered to the department stores and smaller dealers of the city, electrical and electronic merchandise imported from Japan, sewing machines from America and Britain, sports equipment from China and a host of other modern articles from many other countries that Burma was not manufacturing. Demand from the affluent citizenry had been ecstatically encouraging, and Guhan Singh was making a tidy profit from his operation. But that morning, he was nervous. He had been tipped that an all-out operation was underway in the city, and that the junta was making good its threats of abolishing private enterprise.

'We're getting caught at a most unfortunate moment,' he said to his brother. 'What is the value of our current stocks?'

'Over three million kyats,' his brother replied.

'Outstanding?' Guhan Singh asked.

'Around a quarter million due from the local dealers,' answered his brother. 'Thank God, we've diverted the last shipment to our Singapore operation.'

'Thank God, indeed. We would have sunk otherwise,' confirmed Guhan Singh, but as a businessman, he could not bear the prospect of losing an asset that was worth over five million kyats, considering that the three-storied building where he situated his operation was his as well.

'Sir, soldiers have surrounded the building!' a flustered office boy announced, blustering into Guhan Singh's office.

'What!' exclaimed the two brothers, jolted by the mention of soldiers, and rushed to the window.

'Oh my God!' Guhan Singh gasped, looking down at the pavement of his building. There were scores of soldiers—a full company of them, he assessed, their rifles pointing at all the windows of the building.

'What is this for?' he blurted out, recoiling from the window instinctively, and from the glint of the muzzle of a rifle that had stared at him.

'The bastards! Why, we're not criminals!' exploded his brother, the warrior gene in him incensed by the vulgar display of unnecessary force by the regime.

'Please be quiet, Brother,' cautioned Guhan Singh. 'Just play along with them. It's their country, don't forget that. And let me do the talking. Get the accountant because they'll want to see our books.'

No sooner than he instructed his brother, a brigadier of the junta swaggered into his office.

'This company is hereby proclaimed the property of the people. Surrender your books immediately and no one is to leave the building without my permission,' the brigadier declared unceremoniously.

The inquisition had begun with the acquisition of the assets of Guhan Singh and his company. The few big department stores in the city—including the ones in Scots Market—vanished next, along with the stocks and the book-keeping.

A few refrigerators, some electrical appliances, a few sets of radios, an iron or two and several fans left these books and found their way into the homes of the commanders. All of this and more followed in the name of the people. What the people didn't see then was the direction in which these actions were leading. It was the beginning of an ideology getting corrupted.

*

23 February 1963
Rangoon

The Central Bank of India—including 14 foreign and 10 local banks—were nationalized and renamed People's Banks in numerical order 1 to 24. Military officers were installed as general managers of the banks.

'God!' exclaimed Stanley. 'They're targeting the Indians.'

Stanley was dismayed to see the anguished run on the banks in a futile attempt at recovery of jewellery and personal savings by his countrymen. Severe restrictions were imposed. Foreign banks were paid the extent of capital originally brought to the country when establishing, but interest earnings since were not reimbursed. 'People's sweat,' claimed the junta. 'It belongs to the people!' Deposits could be kept only in one account in one bank. Only 10,000 kyats per month not exceeding 50,000 kyats per year could be deposited; no more than two withdrawals per week and not exceeding 10 per cent of the account could be made.

The junta comprised of some bigots who, under absolute power, seized the opportunity to carry out their personal vendetta—which most did. The vendetta against the Indians allegedly originated from a brigadier whose rabid hatred of the Indians finally culminated in the exodus of the Indians from the country.

Further nationalization followed, its tentacles strangling the multinationals and corporations that operated in the country. The petroleum industry, the tobacco industry, the hospitality industry, the entertainment industry, road transport, etc. became state-owned operations. Cinema houses in Rangoon discontinued the screening of Western movies. A genre of Russian movies extolling Soviet virtues assaulted the psyche of the moviegoers. Local studios stopped the production of movies that the junta considered decadent and the industry, impoverished as it was by the lack of adequate equipment, struggled to stay alive with the few state-directed propaganda films.

The face of the country had changed dramatically since 1962; in Rangoon, one now saw jack-booted, armed motorcycle policemen patrolling the streets of the city.

But there were leaders who were better educated and held the country's interest in proper perspective. These leaders disapproved of some of the regime's unsound policies and believed that the abolition of private enterprise at the basic level would paralyse the economy of the country. They advocated a gradual transition to complete nationalization and abolition of private enterprise, which would give the state the time to evolve an apparatus that could take over the smooth running of the nation's economy proficiently.

These few leaders were to pay a price for voicing their finer thinking and conscience. Dissent over policy—economic, political or social—was expeditiously contained.

The Insein Prison—acquiring now an insatiable appetite from a diverse cuisine of a prime minister, petrified politicians, senior abbots, student leaders—was more than glad to oblige the general and his junta by listing a brigadier on its menu.

Aung Gyi!

'Aung Gyi's in jail,' spread the word, and gained credibility because he was considered a moderate among the brigadiers. Substantiation of the rumour came when the papers indelibly reported that Brigadier Aung Gyi had resigned from the army. The paper showed a picture of the brigadier having his head shaved and embracing monkhood. A threat to the oligarchic policies of the regime was isolated felicitously with the veneer of religious sanction.

*

The Cushing High School
Ahlon, Rangoon
1965

The Christian school in the city was well-known for its cadre of dedicated teachers who, under the administration of an able principal, ensured outstanding results from their students year after academic year. Founded by American missionaries, the school fielded a large ground, from the centre of which rose a tall edifice that towered over massive stone buildings three storeys high, that housed the classes and the hostels. This tall edifice chimed the hour and monitored the progress of timetables and the rotation of teachers during the day, while at night it kept watch over the boarders who thronged the school from other parts of the country. Stanley's eldest son, Simon, studied in the school and had expected to graduate from it the following summer.

'Hey Solomon, look,' Simon said, tugging at the sleeves of his friend's shirt, noticing a car and a few jeeps parked outside the principal's office as they entered the gates of the school that morning. A pennant fluttered from the bonnet of the car and the colour of the vehicles was jungle green. The insignia on the pennant suggested high rank.

'It's military!' Solomon exclaimed in surprise.

'What's the army doing here?' Simon wondered aloud in surprise. 'They're probably after you,' he quipped. 'They're catching the Karens, I hear.'

'Oh yeah? They're actually after you. In addition to Karen blood, you've got Indian as well. Double trouble for them…. They've been after half-breeds, you know!' jested Solomon in his repartee.

'Oh. Go on, will you….Wait, they're after the principal,' uttered Simon, somewhat shocked and surprised.

'He's a harmless man, Simon. He could not even hurt a fly,' rebuked Solomon.

'I know. But he's a Karen,' remarked Simon.

'Shit!' exclaimed Solomon. It was true that not only the principal and most of the teachers were Karens, but like him, the school had a large population of Karens—among the other ethnic students.

'Let's not joke about this,' offered Simon in peace. 'There's something going on, more than we can imagine. Let's find out.'

'Probably getting a son or daughter admitted,' remarked Solomon. 'Nothing serious I'm sure.'

'In midterm?' questioned Simon.

Simon's guess was close to the truth. The junta had soon perceived the need to take over the schools to inculcate a generation of students and teachers alike in the values and morals of the dictator's socialism. The large assembly of students on the school grounds for the morning prayer was disallowed, and the practice was now restricted to classrooms. Christian schools in Rangoon now introduced as morning prayer a propitious word to God for the glory of the regime and its ideals. Wearing of Western dress was banned and national dress was made mandatory. The instruction of subjects in English was discontinued and replaced by Burmese. These schools now had high-ranking military officers entrenched in the principal's chambers to enforce the new edict. Cushing School now had a colonel, a non-academic, overseeing political indoctrination.

'Hey, what happened to your Beatle crop, Solomon?' asked Simon one morning at school.

'Knocked it off, what else,' answered Solomon in a foul mood. Solomon had always worn his hair long, like The Beatles, ever since the band from England had became a phenomenon on the air waves and magazines.

'Yeah, I guess you won't stand out that way and bother His Master's Voice,' sympathized Simon. Solomon had been chastised in the presence of the entire class a morning ago for aping the West by the colonel, whom they alluded to as His Master's Voice—a pompous man who now sat in the erstwhile chamber of their principal, downgrading the poor man to an assistant.

'Poor Ginger, she got a mouthful as well,' Simon remarked, noting Solomon's silence. 'All because she's got a pair of prominent boobs,' he added.

Much to the embarrassment of Ginger—an attractive Christian, ethnic Chin girl from the north boarding at the school and a classmate of them—the colonel had reprimanded her for not wearing a loose blouse that would tone down the protrusions from her chest which nature had endowed upon her.

'Shut up, will you Simon?' admonished Solomon. 'You'll get us both in trouble. Remember, he's got his cronies around.'

'I'm sorry, Solomon. The less we talk, the better for us. I guess we're not invulnerable.'

Simon realized that the atmosphere in the school had indeed changed. The excited laughter, the fraternity between the students, the pop culture and fashion had all dissolved into an invidious environment of suspicion and aloofness. One did not talk to anyone unless he or she was a long-standing friend. Western music disappeared from the school socials altogether. Especially after the general—his sleep disturbed one night by a band playing near his residence—stormed in and kicked the drummer and the drums, putting a stop to the party, not without breaking a few guitars before he strode out.

'Hee…hee…hee….So you're the Brahmin of the class now, Simon,' Solomon laughed uncontrollably one evening as soon as they had cleared the gates of the school. Simon had received his share of ridicule that morning when the colonel had picked him to exhibit to the class what a Brahmin looked like, particularly drawing attention to Simon's ears and nose. What was galling was that the allusion to 'Brahmin' was not complimentary, as it was not associated with scholastic ability but an insinuation of the contempt the regime held for Indians. The Brahmin was usually associated with greed and cunning. The joy of schooling was dampened and, except for Solomon and a handful of friends, ethnic and Burmese, Simon began to stay away from associating with a host of other students.

*

Next on the national agenda was the expelling of foreign press across the border and silencing of the national press.

Those who owned radios now listened to the BBC and the Voice of America for news in the confines of their homes, turning down the volume to its bare minimum audibility, while some tuned into radio Ceylon for Western music. None encouraged gossip, nor did they entertain discussion or voiced their opinions, for the people were beginning to learn a new attitude: a distrust of their neighbours. Except for the summer water festival *Thingyan*, when the youth would indulge in splashing water on passers-by and courting future brides, or the festivals of lights *Thadingyut*, when families would illuminate their homes with candles and coloured bulbs and the streets lit by the municipality, displaying ostentation of any sort disappeared from Burmese society. Inconspicuousness became a virtue.

This was thus the epochal change that the general and his junta bestowed upon its people. And while the nationalized and confiscated wealth never reached the people, the army grew aggressively stronger. The general had, in effect, pulled a curtain over Burma—a curtain made of fine green bamboo, sinewy, agile and tough, behind which he could use his army like a whip.

His republic secured and the omnipotence of the Revolutionary Council of Burma now firmly established, the general then turned his attention to the ethnic peoples and their quest for autonomy, for he could now deal with them without interference and distraction. He also turned his attention upon the unfinished work on the foreign companies and the undesirables still in the country. The general's whip then turned on Stanley and stung him with its lash.

*

Far East American Exploration
Burma Office, Rangoon
1966

Far East American was an American oil exploration company based in California licensed to operate in Burma, and had been running a successful operation until the government decided to revoke its license. It was a measure invoked by the junta where they could not resort to nationalization. Chester G. Wallace, the director of the company's operations, was in the city and officially terminating the operations in the country. His team of geologists was flying home in a few days and for all practical purposes, the company would cease to exist in the next several weeks. With help from the American embassy, the director was negotiating with the junta the 80 million-dollar equipment now in the regime's hands. He also needed an arbitrator in Rangoon to follow through the repatriation of funds from the proceeds allowed by the regime.

'I see no one other than you,' said Chester G. Wallace, 'capable of handling the company's affairs to successful conclusion over here, Stanley.'

'Does it mean I still have a job, sir?' asked Stanley. Stanley had been in charge of running the Burma office of the American company since 1960. He had come a long way from his humble beginnings with the Japanese shipping company, and was now drawing a gratifying income. The regime's decision to invoke the license for operations in the country had terminated his corporate ascent at its pinnacle abruptly.

'Call me C.G. That's fine with me,' said the director. 'Yes, for some time ahead, I should think.'

'It could take months, with the way they work here,' commented Stanley. 'The office would have to be closed down, C.G.; in fact, soon after you leave.'

'That I understand,' nodded Wallace.

'How do you suppose I'll function then?' quizzed Stanley.

'I'll have a word with Under Secretary Robert Sullivan from the embassy to provide you with communication facilities. Your reports on developments could be routed through the embassy, as we would your salary.'

'I see,' said Stanley. 'Wouldn't that arouse suspicion?'

'Why should it? You're not a cloak-and-dagger man but a bona fide employee of the company, overseeing pending affairs until satisfactory conclusion,' C.G. countered. 'I'll have you issued with the power of attorney to that effect.'

'That would be found acceptable,' acknowledged Stanley. 'At least for a while.'

'Until then, you're okay I suppose,' observed Wallace. 'If you're not planning to return to India, you should look into citizenship soon, Stan. I sense that India would be safer in the long run. We're all growing old, you know. And Burma will never be an India or allow it to become an America. Remember how the continent became American? My reading is that they aren't too keen on allowing foreigners to stay on in the country for long.'

The company had, in effect, retained him on a contingency basis to oversee its interest and the repatriation of any convertible asset that the government would allow. For the next several months,

Stanley discharged his duties: visiting the American embassy regularly, submitting his reports (typed by Dora at home at night) and collecting his salary. The uneasiness intensified in him as the days progressed, for he became conscious of the fact that he was still a foreigner in the country visiting another foreign embassy to collect pay for his reports, and that a rabid suspicious regime could impute his actions as nefarious.

'Morning, Mr David,' greeted the marine sergeant at the gate as he entered the embassy one morning. Stanley acknowledged the sergeant and proceeded to meet Under Secretary Robert Sullivan.

'Stanley! How's the family doing?' greeted Robert. He had come to like Stanley, and had enjoyed Stanley's parties which he had attended several times when Far East American was operational in the country.

'They're fine, Bob,' replied Stanley, taking the chair that the American official had indicated. 'Here's the last report. There's nothing the government's going to part with. I had to offer the fleet of the company's jeeps to our Burmese agent as good will!'

'Ha! Ha!' laughed Robert. 'What do you plan to do now?'

'It's probably the end for me here, I gather,' answered Stanley. 'It's unlikely that I'll get a job in the country even if I become a citizen, being an Indian and all that.'

'Things have changed dramatically in less than five years, haven't they?' Robert introspected pensively.

Burma would hold no future for him, Stanley surmised. And unless he was granted citizenship, he feared that he would have to leave the country soon. Anti-Indian sentiment was at its peak and the realization tormented him; he thought of his wife and children, saddened that he would have to change their lives and disturb them as well.

*

Stanley's Residence
Insein
9:00 PM

Stanley did not have to wait long to confirm his fears, nor did the state take time to dispel any delusion that he might have entertained in his mind. A week later, just as Stanley and his family had dined, an insistent knock sounded on his door. He wasn't expecting a visitor, but thought nothing of it as he stepped towards the door.

'Must be a neighbour,' commented Dora nonchalantly. It was not unusual for a neighbour to appear at your door in the night to temporarily borrow an urgently needed item. They were still living in a fairly informal neighbourhood of friendly and peaceable folk, composed largely of the ethnic community.

'Yes, probably for something,' Stanley agreed and opened the door with a cordial smile, fully expecting to discharge an exercise in generosity when, to his utter surprise, he found two uniformed men staring into his eyes with serious intent.

'Mr David? Military Intelligence Service.'

A cold shiver raced up Stanley's spine as he heard the chilling introduction of the two MIS officers. 'Yes, gentlemen,' Stanley acknowledged, 'do come in, please. What can I do for you?'

The officers declined the invitation and said, 'Please come with us. We'll wait here while you dress.'

Stanley's jaw dropped, perturbed with the instruction, but he complied without risking another question. He had not committed any felony whatsoever, and thought it prudent to show courage to these two officers.

'Don't worry,' he told Dora and the children. 'I'll probably be late. Don't wait up on me.'

'We'll bring him back,' comforted the officers to Dora, noticing the fear on her face. The assurance sounded kind and uncharacteristic of the MIS, thought Stanley as he entered the jeep the officers had brought to fetch him.

Stanley returned home in the early hours of the morning. It was still dark, for the sun had not yet risen. He was exhausted and shaken but physically unharmed. They had wanted to know what he, a foreign national, was still doing in the country when the company he was working for had already closed down.

They were also interested in his future plans, and particularly curious about his source of income. He had been observed frequenting the American embassy and although they accepted his explanation, they were curious to know whom he knew in a personal capacity in the embassy.

'This is a mild warning, Dora,' Stanley whispered to his anxious wife, not wanting to wake the children up. 'I think it's just the beginning. It's fortunate that they have not insinuated anything as yet on my visits to the embassy,' he said with a measure of relief.

'It still means that you are a watched man, Stanley,' Dora observed gravely.

'No uncertainty about that now,' Stanley agreed. 'It's curious that they didn't ask me why I had not applied for citizenship until now, and were only curious about my link with the embassy.'

'Don't they know about it? What did you tell them?' asked Dora after a pensive moment.

'The truth,' Stanley replied. 'I told them that the company was remitting my salary through the embassy for the duration of my contingency employment, and that my tasks were at an end.'

'Did they believe you?'

'I don't know. I hope they did. Anyway, I've been filing my income tax returns religiously. So that should at least tell them that I have been earning a legitimate salary over here,' answered Stanley with uncertainty.

'Well, even if you happen to be an Indian, they must realize that you're an honest one,' chuckled Dora.

'I think we'll have to leave the country, Dora. I won't be able to stand this harassment, and the last thing I want is to be made an example of by some quirk of fate.'

Stanley had raised the subject of leaving the country on several occasions, but had never pressed the matter sensing that Dora had always been unwilling and reluctant to discuss the issue. He understood the sentiment and could appreciate the strength of family bonds, but had come to the conclusion that he couldn't afford to be delicate or vacillate any more after the interrogation. He was certain that the government knew of the arrangement the company had made with the embassy, and that the visit of these intelligence people was to probe further for any possible clandestine connection he had with it.

'It has to be now or we will never get out. This country is closing down fast, Dora. I personally think they're not going to grant citizenship. They're likely to treat us as aliens…unwanted and probably illegal in due course,' Stanley told his wife sternly.

'What do you plan to do?' asked Dora, half her mind afraid of her husband's answer and the other half sadly preparing to accept the inevitable.

'There's repatriation going on and this will be our last opportunity,' he said in a sad tone, referring to the mass repatriation of his countrymen that the government of India was undertaking at the moment.

'You can elect to stay with your people if you wish, although it might not be wise in the long run. The Karens are as unpopular as the Indians here,' he said, giving her the choice and freedom of will, but also reminding her of her own future prospects in a land where her people were regarded as renegades.

'I understand, Stanley,' Dora answered, recognizing the import of her husband's statement, and knew that the time for a decision had come.

Dora thought of Stanley and the confounding romance that had ignited between them beyond the barriers of culture and creed, beyond the considerations of social politics and racial prejudice to transcend them above such impositions, and reach out at the universality of the species. She thought of him as an unusual man, for it was beyond her understanding how he could reconcile his Christian faith with his perseverance of Hindu philosophy and mysticism. He would sing sonorously with the choir at the Rangoon Baptist Church on Sundays and practice yoga at home in the night when he was not inclined towards copulation. Despite some of his eccentricities and contradictions, she was grateful that he had proven to be an honourable man.

It had taken a few years for her family to recover from their consternation and apprehension over the marriage, she recalled, but had now come to hold him with affection and regard. Even the local pastor who was a Karen had become a frequent visitor at their home, dining with them on many occasions while having long discourses over Christian theology and divergent philosophies. Stanley had also achieved a place of prominence for both of them in Rangoon society, small though it was.

She reminisced fondly about the embassy parties to which both Stanley and she had regular invitations. She particularly enjoyed the evenings when the stream of company personnel from America would occasion Stanley's hospitality at home. They enjoyed her cooking, especially her pork roast! She had enjoyed playing the gracious hostess. And just when everything seemed to be going well, this circumstance, like a vile creature, had pounced on them, threatening to destroy and devour everything they had achieved.

She also knew that before long the Karens would go under the microscope of the regime. There were already many returning to their villages, especially those who had lost their jobs with the foreign companies that were winding down like a string of bulbs switched off one after another. Even her family who were now in Rangoon had finally thought it best that she follow her husband, despite their willingness to provide for her husband, her and her children.

She considered her family's offer again. This was a most difficult choice and was tearing her heart asunder. Her mother, sisters and brother, an entire family tree of relatives, would now only be photographs and letters for as long a future she could see. Returning to or visiting her homeland was not even a vague possibility in the foreseeable future, for she would have to renounce her citizenship to follow her husband.

'Yes. I've made my choice,' she finally said, arriving at a decision after a long, agonizing moment. 'We'll go to your embassy tomorrow, Stanley, and get the papers done.'

'We'll tell the children later in the day,' he said as the first light of dawn crept over the tired couple.

'The younger ones wouldn't understand, but I think Simon's going to be very upset,' murmured Dora as she closed her eyes to the sorrow that was crystallizing in her being.

Her place was with her husband and her children, she decided; for better or worse, in sickness and in health, to honour and to cherish until death did them part. So she had vowed and so she would adhere to it. And with that thought, she rolled down a curtain to veil the attachments of her life in the land where she was born.

A Farewell to Rangoon

Rangoon Harbour
Burma
25 December 1966

Christmas Day. It was an unusual Christmas for Simon because it wasn't the kind of Christmas he had had the past 15 years. There weren't the usual presents or the scintillating Christmas tree, nor were his friends and cousins around. He was not in a home with family but on a ship.

Only Solomon, his best friend in the land, was there standing on the wharf of the Rangoon harbour to bid farewell. Thiers had been a great friendship, and it had hurt Solomon that Simon would not be constantly by his side anymore to grow together into manhood. He had decided to stand on the wharf in the scorching sun that morning, until the eventual moment when Simon would disappear from his vision. His act was an epitome of an endearment that rebelled at the vagaries of life.

Simon missed those few now, Solomon in particular, who had made him feel like he belonged, those few whom he grew up with intimately, sharing the problems of growing up and the illicit excitement of guarding the same prohibitive secrets—secrets which were, in reality, facts of life but would have only earned admonishment from the elders were he to have enquired them as to the nature of his discoveries. The comfort he had enjoyed in the country as an adolescent and a budding youth had ended abruptly.

It was also a significant day for Simon—a day that would change his life forever, a day that would separate him from his mother's land for an indeterminate stretch of time. He was a victim of a new emerging politics, typical of post-World War II South East Asia; a kind of politics that had fuelled in the leadership a sense of nationalism, and a leadership that had aggrandized itself with loot and usurped power while stifling the voice of freedom and rationality in an infant proletariat they had chosen to lead for the many decades that would lie ahead.

'Simon,' his father had said, 'I realize that things will not be the same again, Son. It's a new country, a new people and a new environment. You will have to adapt to it. You might look at me in anger when things don't turn up right, but I think leaving Burma, even under these circumstances, is the best for us all.'

'But why, Dad?' he had asked. 'Mom's folks will take care of us. They have said so…and getting started with a new job shouldn't be difficult, should it?'

It was then that his father revealed to him the nature of political and social consequences. As the son of an Indian father and a Karen mother, his life would have been filled with discrimination and suspicion going ahead. A university education for Simon would have been improbable, and securing a comfortable niche in the new social order unlikely. Worse still was the probability of being influenced by some fatalistic sense of romance or bravado and turning radical, joining the Karen Army at the Thai border, or the misfortune of being gang-pressed into the Burmese Army's slave labour.

It had startled him that his father no longer had a future in Burma. His father was now 55 years old, and at the end of meaningful employment. His mother would have had to leave Rangoon and return to her ancestral countryside eventually, which was fraught with hostilities between the Burmese soldiers and the Karen insurgents.

Had the countryside anything to offer, he wondered, except raring chickens and ducks, pigs and geese? What would they do for rice? Bridges that were blown up by the insurgents and the retaliatory measures resorted to by the government soldiers—claiming its toll on hapless civilians—had also laid to waste thousands of acres of paddy land his mother had a share in. And...no more of the Beatles' songs!

Was it vision, wisdom, paranoia or just human instinct to survive that prompted his father's move? Simon wasn't quite sure then, but there he was, on the deck of the rusty old ship, curious at the void ahead of him that was waiting to be filled.

*

On Board the *SS Saudi*
26 December 1966

The *SS Saudi*, rumoured to have sunk off the Andaman Islands on a timber run several months later, was a decrepit cargo vessel hastily modified to transport a different kind of cargo. The old vessel would now be carrying in its hold an unwanted humanity—human beings, young and old, male and female, families; Indians, ostracized and no longer encouraged to live in Burma, and no longer desired in the new era that was dawning upon the country.

Captain Fernandes watched from the bridge a group of Burmese immigration and customs officials, along with a pilot, board the ship. The captain was not particularly anti-Burmese, nor was he a stranger to the port. In fact, he had visited this port many times during the past several years of his maritime career, and had found Rangoon appealing amongst the various ports he had called on in the South and Middle East; he had known quite a few Burmese on shore to whom he had taken a liking.

But today, Captain Fernandes felt a strong resentment building in him, and he wished that he had the power to throw overboard the party of Burmese officials arrogantly boarding his ship for the final clearance. He was surprised at the developments in the country since 1962 that had changed the demography of the country almost suddenly. The new era in the country was called the Burmese way to socialism, recalled Captain Fernandes; a socialism that, to him, seemed to have punished entrepreneurs with confiscation, a socialism that had invoked a larger political apparatus called nationalization.

'We'll sail immediately as soon as the buggers get off the ship,' he said to his chief, and prepared to meet the approached officials.

'Yes, sir,' acknowledged the chief, himself incensed with the degradation of his countrymen by the very people his government had time and again helped during their moments of crisis, and especially when their government had been threatened by an insurrection in the country in recent times.

The formalities were completed with the fewest of words that rose above the pregnant silence of the ship's crew, presenting the Burmese officials with a stiff atmosphere of uncommunicativeness. Captain Fernandes chose not to ease the discomfiture of the Burmese officials and carried himself just short of rudeness which, to his satisfaction, expedited the inspection. The officials hastily left the ship, their nerves on edge under the sullen glare and the indicting roar of the ship's manifest that their government had deprived of a livelihood, stripping the people of their dignity and self-respect.

Given the clearance by the officials, U Hal Sein—the Burmese pilot on board the *SS Saudi*—navigated the ship through the mouth of the Irrawaddy River and handed over the command of the ship to Captain Fernandes, his job now done. Their eyes met and locked for a moment, sharing a commonality as marine men, uncompromised by the politics of power and racial prejudice. Captain Fernandes extended his hand which was taken warmly by the Burmese pilot.

'I am sincerely sorry to see the misery on this ship,' U Hal Sein said over the firm handshake. 'I never dreamt that Burma would become a dictatorship. It's an aberration to our religion, which is so grounded in compassion, tolerance and peace. Maybe the country is suffering from bad karma,' the pilot offered apologetically.

'I don't know about that, Mr Hal Sein,' replied Captain Fernandes, 'but I suppose there will be some like you whose human values will prevail and hopefully restore this beautiful country again to what it was.'

U Hal Sein smiled at Captain Fernandes but refrained from comment. Pensively leaving the ship, he carefully concealed under his jacket a carton of American cigarettes that the Indian captain had given him. The magnitude of the Indian refugee crisis had stunned him and he was lost for an explanation. Probably their karma was as bad, he thought as the tugboat took him back to the harbour. He looked back at the ship he had just left and felt a guilt he hadn't experienced before. It had made him feel miserable. 'May God go with those unfortunate Indians,' he prayed.

On that day on the Irrawaddy, Dora, too, bore a misery. She bore the misery of severance from her roots and she bore the misery stoically, holding back her tears and waving back at the fading figures of her family at the harbour as the *SS Saudi* began its voyage. It was her turn now to be the foreigner. The ship steamed for six days across the Bay of Bengal: its destination, Madras, South India.

And on that day, leaving a Burma that was metamorphosing into a xenophobic society and still ambivalent about the surrender of his attachments in the land of his birth that the turn of events had necessitated, Simon's unreconciled mind was assuaged by the inducement of new discoveries waiting on a distant shore. The spirit of adventure thrilled him and, for that moment, Simon didn't feel the pain of uproot and sailing the uncharted waters ahead of him.

*

The Bay of Bengal
26–31 December 1966

Except for one still and dark night when the soothing calm of moonlight and the twinkling beacons of the stars were curtained from the sky, there wasn't any cause for apprehension. Throughout the voyage, the usual seasickness was evident on the ship. Captain Fernandes could not help that the food was symptomatic of refugee quality. But he had a great admiration for the Indian government for bringing home her people. Thousands and thousands of them! He had already made half a dozen runs and was due back in Rangoon, and in a fortnight hence, be ready for the final sail to pick up the last group of refugees.

The thought briefly alleviated the captain's moral discomfort over the misery that swamped the ageing ship.

The sea was frequent with a display of its aquatic troupe of flying fish, jubilantly breaking surface and dexterously flying in the air and diving again into the deep blue, momentarily delighting those on-board, while an occasional ship appearing on the horizon would cause ripples of excitement amongst the passengers, only to leave them awash with a sense of hollowness as it vanished like a mirage. Captain Fernandes thought it was, perhaps, symbolic of a cherished past materializing momentarily with stirring clarity in their minds, only to remind them that it was now beyond their grasp forever.

Simon met new friends during the voyage, teenagers like him who had left their attachments behind and whose adolescent dreams had remained unfulfilled. Their first infatuation and crush now only a wistful memory as the *SS Saudi* inevitably distanced their watery thoughts from the land of their birth with miles upon nautical miles of Poseidon's kingdom. These were friends who he wouldn't meet again because, like him, they, too, would become preoccupied with their own survival in the new land but friends, nevertheless, they were for that moment in time. They sang the songs of The Beatles, spoke of the girlfriends they had or had fancied and passed amongst them a few treasured photographs, and vaguely fantasized about the future. They hardly spoke of their personal sorrows and loneliness, or their fears. Instead, they created a bond for that short time they had, filling their moments with fellowship, for they were all fellow travellers 'in the same boat'.

Simon wondered about his father's people, whether they were anything like the baffling human swarm around him…or how they would react to an alien incursion upon their established turf. Images of rampant thievery and beggary said to be a peculiarity of the land dominated his mind above that of the alluring grandeur of an ancient civilization.

Simon strolled along towards the stern of the ship and sat through the evening watching the evanescent wake slowly reclaimed by a silent sea. And for the first time, he felt the pang of abandonment by the land of his birth gnawing at his soul.

A curtain had fallen for him at the Irrawaddy River.

*

New Year's Eve
The Bay of Bengal
31 December 1966

The crew of the *SS Saudi* organized a small affair that night on the deck, and invited a few talents they had scouted for that purpose. They wanted a reprieve from their monotony, and New Year's Eve was opportune enough an excuse to indulge in a little revelry. They kept the liquor to themselves under the express orders of the kindly captain but were generous with the food, which was specially prepared for the occasion.

Simon wasn't surprised that he and his new-found friends were the only talents the crew could find on-board, and was honoured to return the compliment. They played popular rhythms of the times on a couple of guitars that the Burmese customs had allowed to get on-board, and sang songs that stimulated them and encouraged the crew to participate in any that they could. He missed his friend Solomon who was an accomplished guitarist, and was glad that he had handed over Solomon his collection of six thousand stamps as a gift rather than leave it with the Burmese customs. He hoped to keep in touch with this friend.

The crew had their own version of musical prowess and all together, they celebrated and ushered in the New Year with alacrity. There was no mention of a competition until a sailor, perhaps feeling a little more generous but apparently more inebriated than the others, decided to award a sum of one Indian rupee to the best twister among the contestants.

For Simon it was an opportunity to earn, and earn he did… that first Indian rupee.

Across the Bay

Madras Harbour, 1 January 1967

Stanley stood at the bow of the ship, looking at the country he had forsaken a little more than three and a half decades ago in search of an identity his native milieu couldn't offer. From this very port, he had sailed to Singapore with a small suitcase and a wallet that his eldest sister had provided in exasperation so that he could pursue his dreams, and now he was back at the same port with a smaller wallet and a big suitcase full of family: a wife and seven children.

His past identity was now small and irrelevant history that had rolled through time; an icon forged by the winds of change but a relic that few would understand. He set his memories aside as the port loomed ahead, and thought of the tasks awaiting him. He had to get to Bangalore, another southern Indian city, where he hoped his eldest sister would still be a doctor in a hospital.

That had been 37 years ago.

He wished he knew for certain; he regretted that he hadn't kept in touch with her all those years, but there had been the war that had changed his priorities—a war that had led him to Burma, a country that had never been on his mind when he had set sail to discover the mysteries of the Orient East.

*

Madras, South India, 1 January 1967

Simon had no delusion that there would be the Statue of Liberty to feast his eyes upon, or that he was on the *Mayflower* hoping to see a virgin continent that promised paradise. As he disembarked from the bowels of the *SS Saudi,* Simon gawked at the sight of his new countrymen—a sheer mass of humanity that he never knew existed—toiling, chattering and spitting, and generally looking in more dire circumstances than he was in. He couldn't imagine how he would make a living in this land that was going to adopt him?

What was peculiar was that except for several individuals, whom he intelligently assumed to be officials, the majority of the people wore hardly any clothes at all; and that the government didn't seem to mind. Was this democracy, Simon wondered, not oblivious of the Indian government's magnanimity to accommodate them and allow them to set up home on their soil?

Overpowering the pervading stench of stale urea that emanated from some dark corners, compelling and enticing was the spicy whiff of Indian *sambar*, *idli*s, and *vada*s that promised breakfast. The *SS Saudi*'s or the Indian government's decision—he couldn't tell which—had just stopped providing a meal, for he realized that payment would have to be made.

The Burmese government hadn't made it any easier for them either. The entire family was allowed to carry only 180 rupees, about USD 22 then. But Simon had one rupee that he had won on the ship, and decided to make good use of it and relieve his father. He bought breakfast for the family and promptly relinquished his financial status just when he had obtained it. The breakfast had cost one rupee.

That night, the family boarded the Madras mail, on its nocturnal run to Bangalore; chugging and tooting noisily through an endless maze of stations, each looking like the one they had just left. Wherever he looked, Simon didn't cease to be amazed by the mass of humanity and began to notice for the first time a passivity in the people. Or was it some kind of a collective preoccupation with a common fate, he wondered, that they either didn't care or accepted readily the presence of strangers without a qualm?

The Indian psyche was getting interesting and this was just the beginning, Simon guessed. There would be a lot more to learn, of that he was certain. He was no longer concerned with preconceived notions of the nation, but began to look for the quintessence of the ancient heritage of this land that he was travelling through, so unlike the land that he had left eight days ago.

Simon kept awake at night, recollecting stories of his childhood and thinking of his friends, while his ears and eyes assimilated the din of the pulling and pushing crowd—all trying to secure themselves a place on-board the bulging train as it strained its way across fields, villages and towns, its glowering eye seeking for the station of its sanctuary where it would disgorge its burden of men, mail and material and keep its promise yet another time.

*

Bangalore, South India
2 January 1967

Streaks of light, like emissaries from the resplendent realm of the sun, filtered through the expanse of the eastern sky—banishing before them the hosts of the night as the glorious fireball ascended in their crimson wake, heralding another day of giving life and a re-enactment of the creation.

This was just another day amongst the countless millions of days that the earth was traversing through its territory. This sun had seen this young planet evolve from its primeval insignificance through cataclysmic throes that had even made him shudder. But this planet was a survivor and had come of age, and today was a proud planet teeming with an incredible array of life. Oh! What a waste, moaned the sun, that one day this beautiful blue planet would become—just like him, cosmic history. Neither of them had the power to outlast eternity.

But for now, everything seemed well with the planet and except for a few thousand wars here and there, a colossal poverty and hunger and the beastly propensity of the human race for cruelty and destruction, nothing seemed to be out of the ordinary. Humans! A well-developed, curious life form that carried more venom in its kind than a tarantula, thought the sun in awe.

*

The Railway Station
Bangalore City
January 1967

As daylight broke, rising the night over Bangalore, the exhausted Madras Mail limped into the station. The city was a pleasant sight, gardens green and clean as they were then…reminiscent of the way the British had left it. The barracks that housed the British troops had seen a change of uniform, insignia and flag, but the tradition was maintained. Major roads, intersections, parks, buildings, schools and market squares still retained their British names; heroes of the colonial conquest and silent reminders of a powerful empire that had gone into recession.

Stanley gathered his family and the few boxes containing all his worldly possessions, and herded them to the less busy section of the platform. After refreshing the family from the night's tedium, he left the station for the hospital where he expected to meet his eldest sister. It had become a prominent government hospital and was easily located. His spirits began to soar as the taxi drove into the porch, anticipating wonderment at the reunion, for the prodigal brother had returned home.

'I'm sorry, Mr David, Dr Cecilia died three years ago!
No, she never married...stayed single.
Yes, we believe there are relatives here in Bangalore.
Yes! One of her sisters used to visit the hospital...married to a postmaster.
Why not look up the Christian Theological College? She teaches there.'

The discovery that piped into his ears devastated Stanley. His hope of rescue collapsed instantly, leaving him without an inkling of a doubt on finding an immediate solution to a problem that could soon spell disaster. He wondered whether he had exhausted his share of miracles, for he needed one sorely now. There was a family marooned on a platform of a railway station, pinning its self-respect and livelihood on him. He composed himself with all the will that he could muster and prayed for one more miracle. He still believed in miracles, for he was convinced that miracles had always been the essence of his life.

It was late in the afternoon when Stanley returned to the railway station, looking distraught. His family sensed that something was wrong but kept their silence and allowed him to think, for they had implicit faith that whatever the problem was, he had the ability to surmount it. They had a brisk meal at the station's restaurant, while Stanley sought an answer to a problem that he hadn't anticipated.

He was weighing his chances of holding out at the station against the cost of lodging at a nearby hotel when Stanley felt a sudden stillness descend upon the station, portent with an imminent act of God, he thought, and soon the miracle that he was praying for arrived in the form of a policeman. Sub-inspector Dawson was coincidentally strolling through the station, en route to his office for the evening duty he had been assigned. The tall policemen's trained eyes noticed the attire of a woman and her son, who appeared to be the eldest amongst her children. The attire was Burmese! The policeman had served with the British Indian Army in Burma and still spoke a smack of Burmese. Without hesitation, he approached the family.

'*Nay kown yet la* (Are you well)?' he politely enquired.

Stanley understood the policeman's question, but wasn't confident on continuing the conversation.

'You're from Burma, aren't you?' he addressed Stanley while his eyes swept the family with kindred concern.

'Yes,' Stanley replied.

'Are you passing through Bangalore?' enquired the policeman. He had presumed that the family was waiting for a train connection.

'No, this is our destination,' explained Stanley, and soon the story of his sister Cecelia at the hospital emerged. The policeman decided to rescue the family immediately.

'Come with me,' Dawson asked of Stanley, and they didn't return until later in the evening.

The sun had set and the flare of a maroon twilight at the horizon was retreating rapidly as the hosts of the night began reclaiming the evening sky. Soon, the sentinels of the night became visible, reassuring the family with their winks that this part of their ordeal was coming to an end.

A beaming Dawson and Stanley charged into the station, followed by a few porters who loaded the family's luggage atop a taxi. The family was now on their way to a temporary reprieve from the rigours of a nomad's journey. Sub-inspector Dawson had managed to sway the heart of his superintendent, and secured an unoccupied one-room flat for the family. The flat was theirs for two weeks, by which time the superintendent hoped Stanley would be able to settle his family down.

Stanley set out the next morning with the policeman, opening an account with a local bank where he would transfer USD 1,000 that he had wisely saved overseas during his last days in Burma. He then devoted the rest of the day to locating members of his family. Presently, with the network of the policeman's connections, he began to locate several of them—experiencing the turmoil and the strain of re-establishing relationships that had lost their lustre and vitality.

A few of them were delighted, and some concerned, but the majority of them—daunted by the size of Stanley's family—absolved themselves from a needy recognition of their kin. He was an apparition of the past best distanced from. Stanley soon realized that not a single member of his family could provide an avenue for the resettlement of his family, and that he would have to prowl in this jungle alone, looking for succour for himself and his family.

The initial discomfort and strangeness Dora felt on setting foot on a foreign land where the differences in race, language, customs and culture stood out more glaringly than they did in Rangoon began to dissipate with the ever-present struggle—a struggle for survival in a land that was burdened with a stupendous population, striving for existence in an incredible environment of staggering unemployment.

Being married to an Indian and living in Rangoon in a cosmopolitan environment, small as it was, was not the same as being a Karen married to an Indian, living in a city of Indians where the closest resemblance to her race were the few Chinese who ran some restaurants in the city; they had been in India for more than a generation and had their origins in Calcutta. In any event, the erratic family fortune disallowed her from relishing delicacies her palate had relished in Rangoon.

She marvelled at Stanley who, in all those years in Burma, had felt less a foreigner than she did now, or never showed it if he ever did, and took strength from the thought that whatever the circumstances, bad as they were, she had him and the children. They were her world and she wasn't going to fail them. Ignoring the insensitivity of some she came across and the silent snobbery of her husband's people, she made friends with the Christians of the neighbourhood and took up secretarial practice again with a Christian organization.

Stanley had found work in a small industry that took him throughout the vastness of the country and had, for some time, restored a semblance of well-being in the family. The children had recommenced schooling and Simon would be going to university in a couple of years. The period of penury that befell the family was a hard lesson in parsimony, and pocket money was considered an extravagance. But the children trudged to school, uncomplaining of their frugal lunch packs, tolerating the conceit of their more fortunate classmates.

Dora was amused to see that the Indians were also capable of racism; her children were teased and bullied at times for being Burmese. Paradoxically, they had been teased for being Indians in Rangoon. In time, she began to appreciate the diversity of the people, their beliefs, their languages, their social order and their prejudices, their styles and their exotic deities—which numbered more than a thousand to her.

These were a people who had claim to an ancient heritage, remote in time, now lost in the sacred pages of the Vedas, and sadly eclipsed by a generation whose values and way of life did anything but reflect it. The thriving film and entertainment industry did little to embody or rejuvenate this ancient greatness, but further alienated the ethos of the people with the outlandish plagiarism of a culture they had sought to drive away.

But perhaps it was because of the spirits of their ancients, touching her with their wisdom and peace, that she found security in the subterranean kindness and tolerance this new land had. So she went to work every day, boarding a public transport that was usually overcrowded, patenting her national costume and preserving her identity as if to say, 'Sorry folks, I respect the country and am grateful for the kindness in the land, but I am not an Indian.'

They let her be. It was the nation's gift of democracy to her.

'Stubborn Karen!' Stanley would say, and laugh now and then when she refused to learn how to drape herself in a sari. Her resilience drew respect from the few friends she had made. And this resilience was to take care of Stanley when he no longer could work and began to fall ill. He had run out of his share of miracles by then. She and the three older children would shoulder the family's burden for the next 10 years, soaking in eagerly any report on Burma that would appear in the news.

And it did.

The Echo from Thailand

Bangkok, Thailand
1973–1978

Lieutenant Colonel Phuphathna cruised along the district of Pat Pong in the city on his daily exercise in the upholding of the law of the land. An intelligence official, his chief interest was in monitoring the influx of refugees, exiles and dissidents from neighbouring countries into Thailand—particularly Burma. The inflow had been on the incline, and with it, the potential for crime had also increased. Drug trafficking, arms dealings and prostitution were the bane of the phenomena that his country had, in its passivity, tolerated until the authorities of the land had decided to suffer it no longer. He was the instrument to exact stringent measures to stem the decay afflicting the land.

The lieutenant colonel cruised by the dingy bars, the garish nightclubs and the seedy whorehouses—the sort of places where decadent tourists, sex-starved sailors, perverts and the scum of the underworld would haunt for their days' worth of self-fulfilment. He couldn't deny that Bangkok was a city of sin, not less than the other cities of sin on the planet. What infuriated him was that, apart from the cheap entertainment that the world could wallow in while the wealthier patronized its islands like Phuket enjoying exotic holidays, the world was beginning to see it as the capital of sleaze, stalked by poverty that denigrated the magnificence of the land of the Buddha, its benign religion and its scintillating pagodas, maintained by a culture of saffron-robed monks, intrinsic to ancient Siam.

He steered his car out of the district and drove on to the outskirts of the city, where he eventually pulled up by a monastery. He got out of the car and walked towards a shrine to give offerings when he caught sight of a gathering of worshippers, attentively listening to a monk. The monk who was speaking looked genial, which typified a life of disentanglement from the caprice of mortal attachments, but the language he spoke alerted the lieutenant colonel. The language was Burmese! A gallery of faces flashed across his mind until he stumbled upon the identity of the monk. It was the former prime minister of Burma!

U Nu.

'What is U Nu doing here?' Lieutenant Colonel Phuphathna raised the question in his mind. He had been informed that the former prime minister had been released from jail to take up his religious calling, but found it strange that U Nu was preaching in Thailand. He decided against approaching the former prime minister and, instead, drove back to his office. The matter would have to be reported to higher authorities immediately for them to instruct him on appropriate measures to be taken.

His government was tolerant and sympathetic towards the refugees in the country, whether they be Cambodians, Laotians or Burmese—or, for that matter, the Karens, who had been taking the brunt of the Burmese Army's belligerence. While the Thais accommodated them on humanitarian grounds in accordance with Buddhist compassion, they were sensitive to any exploitation of their kindness by these foreign elements exporting hostilities from their soil.

'Are you certain that you saw U Nu?' questioned General Pawa. 'Was he giving a political speech or a sermon?'

'It's hard to say, General, I don't speak Burmese,' replied Phuphathna. 'And I left immediately, thinking that you should know about it.'

'Good. Keep an eye on him and if you suspect any covert activity, let me know immediately,' said General Pawa. 'We don't want a major problem with the Burmese.'

'What if he is making political speeches? Should I arrest him?' asked the lieutenant colonel.

'Let him make a little noise if he wishes to. In fact, let him make more than a little noise, but that's all,' the general advised. 'I like the idea of embarrassing those gargoyles in Rangoon.'

'Very well, General, I'll let him do just that,' complied the lieutenant colonel.

Phuphathna understood the antipathy the general had towards the Burmese. He himself regarded them as barbarians and could not forget that in ancient times the Burmese had sacked and looted the wealth of Ayudhya—the capital of Siam as Thailand was known then—and had defiled the grandeur of the kingdom. And in recent times, the Burmese Army had, on some occasions, strayed into Thai territory in pursuit of the Karen guerrillas—their excuse being the meandering Moei River, known as Tong Yin in Burma, which their confusing natural borders shared.

*

Meanwhile in India

Dora returned home one evening from work most excitedly, and couldn't wait to blurt out the news to Stanley.

'U Nu is in Thailand, and he says he's raising an army to defeat General Ne Win!'

The excitement that bubbled from her was short-lived when Stanley said laconically, 'Dora, it will take more than that monk and his army, if he can raise one, to beat Ne Win.'

'What about the CIA?' Dora asked.

It was a notorious and popular assumption that preceded a reputation in the subcontinent that the CIA was the only bogey behind any subversive activity to topple elected governments throughout the underdeveloped world, and Dora's enthusiasm with the possibility that the CIA would help U Nu restore democracy in Burma reflected not only that sentiment but a wistfulness that it would facilitate a visit to her people sooner than she had anticipated.

'They'll probably give some weapons at the most, but I doubt whether they'll be able to provide the men,' Stanley opined. 'U Nu will have to mostly depend on fugitive students and exiles, and that hardly qualifies as an army, does it?' Stanley asked.

'No, I guess not,' replied Dora as disappointment set in her, displacing the enthusiasm that had robbed her of reason.

'Even the Karens would think twice before they joined him,' Stanley continued, aware that the Karens had taken up defensive positions for a while, and were more concerned about holding on to those positions in the face of a looming new threat.

'Why do you say that?' asked Dora. 'They still remain opposed to the regime in Rangoon; they've not signed any truce with the government.'

'True enough, Dora,' replied Stanley, 'but you must realize that the teak jungles have always been the haven of the guerrillas all along, shielding them with its thick foliage and deterring the Burmese Army from hot pursuit.'

'Yes, I see what you mean,' commented Dora. 'Is it the Burmese Army selling thc teak to Thai contractors or are the Karens doing it for revenue?'

'It's also a question of Karen sovereignty. Either way, the Karens could lose their sanctuary if the trees are cleared, exposing them to the Burmese Army which has largely been cautious enough to keep away,' Stanley observed.

After a few incidents of being lured into its labyrinthine death traps with calamitous consequences, the Burmese Army had had to review their strategy and before long, Stanley read in the papers about the sale of the teak. The dragnet was closing on the Karens who were now digging in.

'Yes, you're right Stanley,' Dora conceded, 'they'd know better than to risk an ill-founded venture at this time.'

Dora realized that she had not heard of a major Karen exploit that made the news, except the accounts in Thailand of the bloody riots in Rangoon against the Chinese and the crackdown on the students again in 1974. It was no longer the KNDO now, she recalled. The sagas of the sea princes and the Alexanders were over. It was now The Karen National Liberation Army defending themselves in earnest. They were past the purpose of liberation.

Newsweek or *Time,* she recalled, had once run an article with colour photographs, the insightful lens of the cameraman graphically capturing in makeshift bunkers and bivouacs, a people: men, women and children enduring a Burmese shelling with nothing more than a fierce determination to hold on to their little hamlets and their dream. She remembered how for days she had carried the magazine, empathizing with her people, their terror and suffering when the deluge of motor bombs exploded about their little bunkers, while mothers tried to soothe the frightened, wailing children.

'Well, there's dinner to be made,' she said, shrugging the pang of anguish for a family that she had left behind, and prepared to tackle the last chore of the day. Was theirs a lost cause, she wondered...the question weighing heavily in her heart as she entered the kitchen.

It was the beginning of the end of unchallenged ethnic supremacy on the borders of the country. Ne Win's Tatmadaw was getting stronger, and the general, older and more domineering; the infantry remained young, with the induction of fresh indoctrinated blood. Their armouries were now swelling with weapons procured from certain northern neighbours—the Israelis and USSR satellite countries. Ne Win even had a refurbished air force of some squadrons of modernized World War II spitfires and several helicopters, not to be feared by their neighbours but potent enough to change the game on their domestic chessboard.

So when U Nu, the former soft-spoken prime minister, announced to his captors that he was renouncing political ambitions and would spend the rest of his life as a monk, they had released him from prison. True to his word, U Nu became a monk and had started preaching Buddhism to the populace at large, travelling the distances to spread the message of non-violence and non-attachment, much to the delight of the generals. The monk then suddenly disappeared from Burmese soil and appeared in Thailand—no longer a monk but a warrior now, threatening to overthrow Ne Win and his junta.

Ne Win and his junta laughed, a little embarrassed perhaps that the monk had foxed them, but not in the least perturbed by military confrontation. U Nu's rhetoric was a bark without a bite, a nuisance across the border that they tolerated and, in 1980, the junta allowed him to return to the country on the promise that he would strictly adhere to a religious life. U Nu had turned around to become monk-like again. Meanwhile, Ne Win's army commenced consolidation of their ground for the long-awaited offensive against the Karens and other ethnic peoples.

And along with the dissipation of U Nu's threats, Dora's hope of seeing her people vanished into the closet of her imagination. In early 1977, she received the news of the death of her mother and, later in the year, the death of her two elder sisters. In a cascade of silent tears, her spirit accepted the inevitable. There was a time for everyone to die, the Bible had said, but the pain lingered in her heart and she was not to find the balm of comfort for long.

In 1978, Stanley died.

The death of Stanley had impacted upon the family in different ways, varying in intensity and desolation, but was hardest upon Dora. It seemed to have wrenched away from her the zest for life. The death itself was violent and rude. A cancer that had a primary origin in the stomach, routed its secondaries through lung and lymph nodes through periods of dormancy and malignancy.

It had ravished Stanley beyond any hope of remission, despite the care the cancer hospital had provided. How his father had borne the early spasms and preferred not to seek medical attention in order to avoid the expense distressed Simon tremendously, hounding his conscience with guilt whenever his thoughts returned to a heritage that now lay in the ground. What awed Simon was that no amount of sedatives could keep the excruciating pain from savaging the withering body in the last days. It was as if all the bullets and the bayonet thrusts that Stanley had escaped during the War had found their elusive victim with a vengeance, unmerciful and unrelenting in their frightful assault.

'God! Cure him or take him!' Simon had yelled in anger at the sky the night before Stanley died, no longer able to see the banal suffering and indignity of a friend and a father. God seemed to have understood Simon's anger and sent the angel of death the next morning to relieve Stanley from the fathomless agony of living. And in the serenity of death, a curtain call had come, ending the hostility that the cancer had declared upon Immanuel Stanley David.

The Lotus in Rangoon

A Neighbourhood of the Shwedagon Pagoda
Dagon, Burma
1755

Born Aung Zaya, 'victorious' in Burmese, King Alaungpaya reined his mount and imperiously signalled his war-weary troops to an abrupt halt. Frightened of him more than the enemy, the 10,000 men that made his army came to an alert standstill. Wondering whether the king suspected an ambush, the troops, in keen anticipation, waited in silence for the next sudden command the king would issue. The king was known for his acute tactical sense in battle, and despite his unbiased ruthlessness in dealing with slovenly soldiers who failed to rally to his order, the body of men loved and worshipped their monarch who stood tall at five foot eleven inches. Since the beginning of their history, no Burman had ever been able to boast about the incredible successes in battles against their enemies and the extent to which their empire had swollen.

But the king did not issue the anticipated command.

Alaungpaya, meaning 'the future Buddha', was meditating on the past and the rise and fall of dynasties in his country.

The early Pyu, a priestly caste from Northern India, were the earliest who migrated to Burma. Their tradition was deeply rooted in the yoga system from Patanjali and his Yoga Sutras. They established a highly peaceful Hindu kingdom in the Irrawaddy valley around 500 BC. They were also known to practice different forms of yoga such as Raja yoga, Karma yoga, Tantric yoga, Hatha yoga, Dhanda yoga, Letha yoga, Longi yoga and others. They refined the Hatha yoga system, along with the other systems, and created the Hanthawaddy yoga system.

Later, in 250 BC, city states emerged, consolidating the Pyu kingdom. The Pyu had three prominent city states among the score in the country. The oldest of the three cities was Beikthano (the Burmese word for the Hindu god Vishnu), and the other was Sri Ksetra. It was among the Pyu that Buddhism took a deep hold.

The Pyu, predominantly vegetarian, discouraged killing and revered the lives of all creatures, great or small. They created an agrarian society complete with sophisticated systems of canals, elaborate irrigation devices and advanced methods of animal husbandry. The Pyu kingdom became one of the major trade routes between India and China.

Around AD 6th century, the Mons—a fierce warrior people originating from Eastern India—gradually moved down and subdued the Pyu kingdom, and settled in the region. Pyu culture was assimilated by the Mons, who named their domain Hanthawaddy.

What was Pyu metamorphosed into Mon.

Then the Bamars, his people—the earlier Burmans of the Tibeto-Burman strain—migrated to Burma from the Nanzou kingdom, known later as Yunnan in AD 9th century. Living near the Pyu and the Mon at Pagan, the Burmans of Pagan enriched themselves with Pyu–Mon culture. King Anawratha of the Bamars then fought the Mons, defeated them and founded the Pagan Empire.

In 1279, the Tai people were driven out of the highlands of Yunnan by an empire building Mongols. The Tais, who later became known as the Shans, invaded Burma, scattering the Burmese. Pagan declined and the kingdom split into small kingdoms. Thadominbya founded a new kingdom as the rightful successor to Pagan in 1364, in an attempt to reunify the Burmese, and made Ava, officially known as Ratanapura, the City of Gems, its capital. After his death at 21, the court of Ava constantly waged wars with the Shans in the north and the east, the Rakhines of Arakan in the west and with the Mons who broke away from Pagan and founded their Hanthawaddy kingdom in the south. An exhausted Ava fell to the Shans in 1527.

In January 1555, King Bayinnaung of the *Taungoo dynasty conquered Ava. But with the death of the king in 1581, the dynasty declined.*

In 1740, the Mon people began a rebellion. The Mons had restored their Hanthawaddy kingdom at Pegu, their armies aided by the French East India Company, which gave firearms. With the help of Dutch and Portuguese mercenaries, they captured Ava in 1752, ending the 266-year-old Taungoo dynasty.

It was then that he, Alaungpaya, a man possessed with great diligence and vigour, decided to carve for himself an illustrious place in the annals of the Yazawins, the chronicle of Burmese kings. Ignoring pleas from his family to submit to the Hanthawaddy kingdom, he rallied villages, declaring, 'When fighting for your country, it hardly matters whether there are only a few or many with you. What does matter is that your comrades have true hearts and strong arms.' He routed the Hanthawaddy army of Mons, also known as the Talaings, and reunified the fragmented kingdom of Pagan. In his crusade to re-establish Burmese supremacy, Alaungpaya had settled the score with the Shans in the north, stemmed the century-old Siamese incursions, and had savagely routed the Mon powerbase in the south—killing tens of thousands of Mons, including learned three thousand priests, pregnant women and children. A thousand more priests were killed in the countryside. Alaungpaya's army was hugely supported by the British Army, typical of their colonial interest against the French and the Portuguese.

Alaungpaya then founded the Kounbaung dynasty in 1752, last of the Burmese, and created the second largest empire in history—a breakaway from the earlier kings of the Pyu, the Mons and the Pagan kingdoms. But on that day, Alaungpaya—villager, hunter, patriot, warrior, leader, general, conqueror, and dynasty-builder—was suddenly overpowered by a native stirring of the villagers again.

As a villager, he had always loved pristine nature. Bewitched by the tranquil call of the idyllic countryside, unblemished by the sight of hovering vultures, Alaungpaya then decided that the time for hostilities was over and that he would build a city where he had commanded his troops to halt that day in May of 1755. In the peace that befell him, he decided to name the place 'Yangon', meaning the 'end of conflict'.

But the Yangon of Alaungpaya was not to see the end of conflict as was proclaimed by the king.

Yangon was destined to be bathed in blood.

*

The First Anglo-Burmese War
The British Garrison
Rangoon
1824–1825

The British called Alaungpaya's Yangon, Rangoon. War had been declared on Burma by the British, and Rangoon was now in the hands of the British. The few guns the Burmese possessed had been surprised and tamed. The city had fallen quickly and the British garrison was waiting for the Burmese counter-attack.

The Burmese troops, arrayed for the counter-attack on the city to evict the invading colonial British, were an excitable medieval army. They had every reason to be spirited, for they were led by the bravest of their generals—Maha Bundula, who had already had a string of successes against the British in the northern campaign since the declaration of war in early 1824. Bundula's astonishing military prowess during the campaign forced the British to make a strategic change necessary in the conduct of the war: the British decided on a thrust at Rangoon with a flotilla of warships up the Irrawaddy. And here on the banks of the river, General Bundula had decided to stem the tide of the invasion and dispatch the British to their borders in shameful defeat. A fine horseman, the general galloped along the ranks of his infantry, flashing his gleaming *daah* and exhorting his troops to roar—raising their pennants high in the air, challenging the British and eager to engage the enemy in combat.

Major General Sir Archibald Campbell, the commander of the British forces, saw the glint of the general's *daah* and heard the roar of the Burmese troops, recognizing that the Burmese were now prepared to charge. They had the numbers with them and realized that if the force before him were ever allowed near to engage in close combat, his forces would be annihilated.

But the British commander was not unduly worried. He would keep the distance between the two opposing forces until it was the right moment to engage the Burmese. He hoped, however, that the Burmese would charge and give him an excellent opportunity to devastate them with his tactical advantage. He had the Congreves with him. The Congreves were solid fuel rockets which had a range of a thousand yards. Finally, he had the cannons of the flotilla, in addition to the ones at the garrison, and a well-trained and disciplined force.

'Commence firing,' he ordered in a detached tone when, as he had expected, the Burmese horde charged. The naval guns of the British flotilla joined in—their muzzles flashing in a thunderous crash to flash again in another lethal volley, while his musketeers, in the classic triple line formation, stood ready for their orders to rake the approaching defenders with their shots. The determination, the zeal and the courage of the Burmese were torn apart in disarray as limbs flew and bones disintegrated amidst the savage explosions. And soon, they were vanquished.

Shaken with disbelief at the fierce bombardment, General Bundula ordered the retreat and began building stockades on the river, from where he would watch the white barbarians and their awesome warships that had made him eat humble pie. He had announced that he would feast on rice in Rangoon by the end of the week. Bundula, dismayed at his first-ever defeat in battle, soon died on the banks of the Irrawaddy while on a lookout position on a pipal tree. A British cannonball had exploded near his lookout, killing the general instantly and ending the efforts of the Burmese to deny the British the conquest of Burma. Rangoon eventually became the new capital of colonial Burma.

Rangoon continued to see conflict and bloodshed into the second and third colonial British wars, the Second World War and the post-independence era when ethnic peoples of the country revolted with the Karens.

*

Rangoon
1974–1988

Two centuries later, the British or the Japanese were no longer causes of conflict in Rangoon, and the eradication of ethnic insurgency was almost a conceivable certainty. But now the city and the country were in the throes of a much more frightening conflict, jolting the generals of the revolutionary council of 1962. Gross and ill-educated management of the country's economy and the lack of constructive critical review in the face of Ne Win's authoritarianism had finally plunged the country into a miasma of simmering discontent, which flared in a violent outburst, for the people were now fighting for the most essential of substance that allowed dignity and a sense of well-being in a human society—food.

Beginning in May 1974, a wave of strikes hit Rangoon and elsewhere in the country against a backdrop of corruption, inflation and food shortages, especially rice. In Rangoon, workers were arrested and troops opened fire. But the hunger of the people disregarded all forms of fear and imploded within their society, discarding all norms of civility and respect. Burmese began killing Burmese, the strong looting the poor, and together, the ravisher and the ravished uniting to attack government enterprises in their craze to feed the hunger. Fires raged across the country, massacres spread, inmates of prisons revolted and were butchered and the country tilted on the hinge of anarchy.

In 1974, the Revolutionary Council held the first general election after 12 years and, dissolving the council, brought direct military rule to an end. Ne Win was no longer the chairman of the Revolutionary Council but the self-elected president of the single party to contest the election—'The Burmese Socialist Program Party'. Still the omnipotent chairman, he began shuffling his deck of cards, contemplating upon a solution that would appease the people and quell the inferno of agitations across the land. He found the solution—a solution that would also perpetuate his power for life while he remained inaccessible and protected in the background.

He handed out to the people his resignation in 1981 as president of the ruling party, but remained in control of the party and the junta. Despite installing a civilian in the interim period in early 1988, his attempt to appease the people failed to quell unrest. The damage and the hurt that had been caused had sunk deep into the national consciousness, birthing voices of dissent that sprang resoundingly from former members of the Revolutionary Council—like Brigadier Aung Gyi and General Tin Oo. The voice of former Prime Minister U Nu surfaced again, joining those of the deposed army officers, in their attempt to wrestle from the civilian the key to form an interim government and set a precedent for free and fair elections that could herald the dawn of civilian governments in the future.

There was another voice, feminine but resolute; a voice that was determined to seek to the end the cleansing of a nation from its evils that had set in since the past two and a half decades. It was the voice of the little girl who had lost a father forty-one years ago tragically.

The Lotus in Rangoon. Aung San Suu Kyi.

*

A Residence on the Inya Lake
Rangoon
July 1988

'What!' exclaimed the septuagenarian chairman, and demanded, '…when did this happen?'

'Just this morning, sir,' replied his aide, unnerved by the chairman's explosion.

'She's supposed to be here to take care of her ailing mother!' he shouted in consternation. 'We should have watched her from the very beginning. I knew there had to be more than just the visit to her mother.'

'Her mother is really ill, sir,' vouched the aide.

'That I know,' said the retired chairman and continued, 'what I'm surprised about is how she managed to get functional so soon. I'm sure there is some kind of organization without which she couldn't have held a meeting on her own. The bitch!' The jolt that provoked former chairman's harangue had come from a source he had least suspected. He had tolerated the criticism and the squawk for political and economic reforms from her, and had dismissed it as girlish impetuosity in Western intellectual parlance. A spoilt brat was what he had thought of her. He had been watching Aung Gyi, Tin Oo and that infernal U Nu who had the audacity to state that he hadn't dissolved his legitimately elected government and, therefore, had sovereign claim to the prime ministership of the new government.

This sudden shift to centre stage under the opposition's limelight meant, to the shrewd septuagenarian, a shift in the opposition's strategy which had to be immediately countered. The legitimacy of U Nu was now a vague contention, and of no great consequence to the people; nor did he believe that the people would die for Aung Gyi and Tin Oo. But the woman was a different matter. She was the offspring of the founding father of the nation...a hero and a martyr fawned upon with exalting poetry and song.

'*Setko July, Mamyitnaing...*' meaning that 19 July of the calendar could never be forgotten, for the assassination of Aung San had occurred on that date. It was literally an emotional patriotic poem, immortalizing her father. The emotional hold she could have on the people was a power that she could wield, challenging the duplicity of the regime's own extolling oration of her father and the exhortations in their address to the nation for their own selfish political ends.

'Get me the intelligence chief immediately. Now!' he rasped and sent the aide scurrying from his lounge. The chairmen then reached for his telephone and dialled the number of the next most powerful man in the country after him. He dialled for the senior-most general of the army, a trusted ally who had seen through the revolution along with him.

*

The Intelligence Chief's Residence
Rangoon

Major General Myo Mint was strolling in his garden, inhaling the fragrance of the jasmine that hung in the fresh morning air, when the aide of the chairman stumbled upon him, gasping for breath and speechless for a moment from his speedy errand.

'General, the chairman wants to see you immediately,' he announced as soon as he recovered his breath.

'Oh! I thought something drastic had happened,' said the intelligence chief in relief. The past few months had weighed heavily on him for, amidst the chaos of changing governments and rumours of the chairman's flight from the country, he had been on constant watch for himself. He knew that the power one enjoyed under a dictatorship was like a finely honed razor that could cut both ways. The frenzy of the aide had worried him and made him think that death had befallen the chairman.

Like many of the men of power in the country, he took refuge in the former chairman's continued span of life, for it ensured them theirs.

'It's Aung San Suu Kyi, sir,' blurted the aide. 'She has given a speech outside her residence.'

'What speech?' asked the general, instantly alert.

'She has declared the formation of some kind of league to restore democracy in the country, sir,' replied the aide.

'What! What league? What democracy? Speak up, man!' demanded a stunned intelligence chief. This was worse than drastic, the shaken general now feared. A major development in the opposition camp that he hadn't anticipated. Was this failure to be fatal? With those worrisome thoughts, he hastily left for the chairman's residence with the aide.

Meanwhile, in the residence on the Inya Lake, the ageing chairman paced the lounge irritably, clasping his hands and trying to gain an insight into the sudden development in his capital. Was this a precursor to something more portentous, like a sudden Western interest in the country, he wondered. Why did she want to get involved in the country's politics when she was married to an Englishman and had a comfortable life in London? Or did she? What about her sons? Or was this an orchestration of some frustration, expressing a need to call attention upon her… or was there some ulterior motive in her attempt at defiance of the regime's rule? Surely, she was educated enough to know the consequences of meddling with him! Was her husband somehow involved in this? Preparing an international stage? The rush of thoughts in the chairman's mind came to a halt when his aide and Major General Myo Mint burst into the lounge.

'I say, Myo Mint, what is this that I hear?' shot the chairman. 'How could you let such a thing happen? It's a good thing that she didn't get to the radio! You're the intelligence chief, for God's sake….And all those people, I believe a crowd…more than a thousand listening to her! Where did they come from?'

'I'm surprised myself, sir, but I'll get to the bottom of it, I assure you,' responded the intelligence chief. It was his misfortune to have being caught napping on this one, but as the person in charge of intelligence, he knew he would have to ride out the chairman's indignation and lambast.

'You must!' enforced the chairman.

'It was very difficult to foresee this, sir. She's the daughter of Aung San! She's like family,' the intelligence chief said, taking the opportunity to minimize the damage caused to his credibility.

'Not anymore,' declared the chairman.

'Who would have thought it appropriate to place a watch on her?' the major general reinforced his defence.

'We have been lax with her and I can't blame you entirely, Myo Mint. We had thought better of her, I agree,' the chairman offered. The wily chairman was notorious for extending an olive branch after remonstrating his officials, and this was the very same olive branch extended to him now, the intelligence chief reckoned. He was still the donkey while the chairman held the whip.

'I want a watch placed on her immediately; what she does, where she goes, who visits her—everything, including all members of her household,' the chairman ordered.

'Very well, sir. I'll get to it right now,' said the intelligence chief in a firm voice.

'Good, Myo Mint. I want a constant update,' the chairman said. 'Get going, then.' Dismissing the major general, the chairman then waited for the arrival of the army commander-in-chief, General Khin Maung Nyunt.

*

Aung San's daughter had come to Burma earlier to look after her ailing mother and, in the time that she had spent in the country, had come to witness the extent of the nation's deterioration. It was no longer debatable print in the newspaper that she read but an empirical knowledge that she gained. She was repelled by the oppression of the regime. Aung San Suu Kyi was angered by the debasement of a people for whom her father had sought liberation. This was not the Burma Aung San had died for, and she was determined to see that her father's death would not be in vain.

Aung San Suu Kyi decided that it was time to flush the generals down their cesspool of corruption, deceit and usurpation of a people's trust. The cry from a daughter of the nation for the liberation of her people from tyranny now rang louder in the chairman's ears than all the gunfire his Tatmadaw had discharged upon the dogs, the students and the insurgents of the country. What galled him most was that it was a woman who, under his unsuspecting nose, had become an anathema to his personal empire. She was demanding for free and fair elections!

'Let us have a dialogue with her, Mr Chairman,' General Khin Maung Nyunt proposed within the first few minutes of his arrival. 'We have a delicate situation here and the sentiments of the people have to be considered before we act. We have to think of the army, too.'

The general's counsel was well-appreciated by the chairman, who himself did not want to precipitate another spate of nationwide censure of him. He was also sensitive to international reaction at this juncture, which could jeopardize his plans for the future that were yet to be announced.

'Yes, I can understand that. Lead a delegation and have this dialogue with her,' the chairman consented. 'Find out what she has in mind. Entreat her, persuade her; appeal to her that it is not in the country's interest to bow to her wishes or to her movement.'

'I will, Chairman,' assured General Khin Maung Nyunt.

'Prevail upon her that it is us who have held the nation together all these years. Our people do not know how to conduct themselves in a free society. They need a firm hand to rule them and if we remove ourselves from authority, she will have to account for the lawlessness that will reduce whatever is left of this country to unimaginable chaos. Look at what's happened recently. Insurgencies rearing their heads again! Threaten her if you have to,' the chairman advised.

'That, I will,' assured the commander-in-chief of the army.

'Promise her, if you must, that elections can be considered when the stability is restored in the country,' the chairman directed. 'A military retaliation will not be in her interest now because we can outlaw any kind of opposition. Tell her to keep quiet in her own interest. Remind her that the army shoots to kill.'

But Aung San Suu Kyi was not to be entreated, nor dissuaded or threatened from her stance despite the fervent overtures of the government to pacify her. Her fortitude lay in rekindling a long-lost courage among the people. In the days that followed, the National League for Democracy (NLD) gained a following, burgeoning by the hour, and the civilian heading the current government was showing signs of cracking. The generals now feared the popular sentiment of the people infecting the younger cadre of their Tatmadaw. It was time to rectify the situation before it went out of hand, and the last thing the generals desired was a mutiny of the younger officers and soldiers. They warned their mentor about the impending debacle, and soon, a meeting was convened.

'Bring in the butcher,' he ordered.

The Lacquered Curtain

Office of the Commander-in-Chief
Military Headquarters
Rangoon
July 1988

The retired chairman sat in the chair from which he had seized the office of power over the land. He looked gravely at the gathering of the generals before him, who seemed like little chickens scurrying to the protective wings of their mother. He was glad that they needed him.

'Comrades,' the chairman addressed the gathering, dispensing with the usual formalities that went with these meetings. The tone in his voice reflected a concern that had set in. He wanted an immediate solution to the menace of Aung San Suu Kyi, before the present government buckled under pressure to her.

'We have to act now before this nonsense of democracy affects our troops.' The chairman was direct and to the point. He didn't believe in an ambiguous play of words.

'We understand that the situation is volatile,' replied a general promptly. They were as concerned as the chairman of the portent of Aung San Suu Kyi's call for democracy, and knew that once they lost the loyalty of the troops, they didn't have a chance.

'If the league ever came to power, they would arrest all of us,' predicted another. The generals might have taken karmic consequences lightly in their next births, but they were not prepared to surrender their present life to an inquisition by a people they had abused.

'We have far too much blood on our hands,' observed another senior officer, who was in charge of law and order with the current civilian government.

'I'm sure they'll indict us with a whole lot of charges,' voiced one of the generals heading the Ministry of Finance.

The generals also feared that, apart from political and humanitarian crimes, they would also be held accountable for economic crimes. The economic collapse of the country had forced them to trade in teak and elephants for immediate revenue. Industry and commerce had languished with atrocious mismanagement, and sanctions against the country's few exportable commodities—including chilies by certain nations—were getting difficult to circumvent. Worse still was the fact that, although once described as the rice bowl of Asia, they now had nothing to export. They were importing!

'Gentlemen,' the youngest of them, heading the Ministry of Education and Cultural Affairs, then raised his hand for attention, 'the problem is that our sister is the daughter of Aung San!' he reminded them.

The misgiving in his statement was shared by all at the meeting, and was the only factor in their consideration that hindered them from resorting to the old tried-out method to which they had become accustomed. The people's adulation of Aung San Suu Kyi was reviving in the people the memory of General Aung San, which made her invulnerable.

'What about international reaction?' asked a councillor in command of the Ministry of Information and Broadcasting.

'She is yet to acquire media significance abroad. If we act quickly and shrewdly, we can contain their interference,' replied the general heading the Ministry of External Affairs.

'This is purely an internal matter and we have the right to handle a domestic problem the way we see fit,' offered the intelligence chief. 'Other countries do it, and so can we.'

'Yes,' acknowledged the army chief, 'but we need to be a little more subtle.'

'The Americans weren't subtle with their native Indians, nor with their Negro slaves,' remarked the intelligence chief. 'And don't forget the English; they're as ruthless with their Irish.'

They were all voicing their apprehensions, the chairman noted with satisfaction. Like him, none of them believed that the party of Aung San Suu Kyi would adopt an attitude of reconciliation. The NLD would have their hardliners as well, who would take the opportunity to seek retribution, the council members feared. They most dreaded the spectre of personal scores being settled in the Insein Prison.

'All right!' interrupted the chairman, rapping the table with his knuckles and silencing the deliberations of the delegation of generals. 'I have discussed the matter at length with General Kin Maung Nyunt and General Myo Mint, and we have pieced together a plan. First, I will retire. I will resign from the party and the junta.'

He had deliberated assiduously for hours on end with the two generals, concocting a profusion of strategies and rationale, gleaning, rejecting and retaining the plausible in the search for a solution to a problem that had caught them off guard. They needed a ploy which, when applied, would appear to be reasonable to the lay public and minimize their aggravation, and possibly pre-empt international criticism. The three had decided that the actions of the council of generals had to appear legitimate, as if dealing with a matter of national security. Eventually, the architects of oppression had pieced together a plan to squash a common threat that came from a lotus, which had chosen to push through the muck of moral stagnation and claim a place under the sun for her people. The plan was simple.

'Comrades, we'll stage a coup! But we need her to lead circumstances to it,' the chairman announced. 'We will have the Butcher to replace the current civilian in office. Yes...the Butcher. We have pleaded with her to abandon her political ambitions, but I'm afraid we have failed. Regrettably, she will continue her demand for multi-party elections and the folding of this government. There are bound to be further meetings, of that I'm sure.

'Now, we will let her have a couple of meetings in order to uncover her sympathizers and wait for the moment when the crowd gets larger, giving General Myo Mint an opportunity to plant his agents amidst them.

'What we have to do is to identify the machinery that is supporting her. Any perceivable foreign involvement would be wonderful because we need not go any further. We crush her party immediately.

'In any event, even if we fail to perceive a foreign hand in her movement and, therefore, cannot discredit her movement, I expect that, due to our passivity, these meetings will get larger, noisier, and hopefully unruly.

'That is the moment when the army will promulgate martial law immediately, citing disturbance of public peace as justifiable cause,' the chairman expounded.

This, he calculated, would take care of the students whom he foresaw as the vanguard of the movement. It was always the students and the intelligentsia all over the world who were problematic, thought the chairman sourly. His eyes narrowed in fury at the thought of the students.

'In conjunction,' the chairman continued, 'we will paralyse the people with the fear by a massive presence of the military wherever sister Suu Kyi organizes her meetings, ostensibly, of course, to prevent violence or riots and destruction of public property.'

This, he reasoned, would alienate and discourage the general public from active support of the democratic movement. There would be many who would recall the shooting of the dogs, the students and workers in his time, he was sure and grinned with satisfaction. He had taken great pains to impress upon his fellow countrymen that Buddhism, a profound religion as it was, had no hold on an army, and that he would not hesitate to let loose its dogs of war on the people at the slightest provocation.

'General Myo Mint's men will instigate and encourage confrontation during these curfews from behind, and the officers of the Tatmadaw must be given to orders to shoot. That will be the Butcher's job! There has to be a shooting so terrifying that it must numb the will of the people. Do you understand?' the chairman demanded of General Khin Maung Nyunt, flailing his fists wildly in the air as traces of spittle flew from his mouth.

'After the shooting, a new cabinet must be formed within forty-eight hours, ease out the Butcher, consolidate your leadership and legitimize army rule,' the chairman instructed. 'Call it the State Law and Order Restoration and Council or Committee, whatever, it doesn't matter, but that entity will be all-encompassing and will control everything in the country. In short, it will bring back the Tatmadaw in direct power.

He had nominated a successor to the current failing government, an avid hardliner who would remain unyielding and steadfast in the execution of the plan.

'The committee will then agree to the people's demand for elections at a convenient time, alleviating their aggravation, and will proffer an invitation to this so-called NLD to participate,' the chairman said.

'Then we will churn up the media,' he propounded, looking at the general in charge of the Ministry of Information and Broadcast.

'The media will be under complete control of the state's law and other restoration council or committee, and will start a propaganda campaign against sister Suu Kyi and her party—alluding to her British connection if we haven't established any foreign involvement by then, and insinuate that she is a tool of foreign imperialist working for the destabilization of our country.'

'General Myo Mint will have, by then, identified the leaders of her party for special treatment, and coerce them into denouncing her or quitting her party. His men will eliminate the fastidious ones,' the chairman stated, and sat down exhausted after his tirade on the anatomy of terror.

'We shall see, then, who will win the elections,' he contended.

The generals were in accord. The chairman was certain that the plan would seal the loyalty amongst them, for each of them needed an exit from this predicament as much as he did. He was satisfied that they would implement the plan to the letter. Reposed with his authority and power again, he relaxed into the chair, but he had not finished yet. The tense creases around his mouth broke into a malevolent grin before he announced his *coup de grace.*

'There is another matter to be taken care of,' he said. The generals propped in their seats attentively, evincing their unabashed chauvinism for the chairman.

'You see, every time people want to run away from us,' he said sagaciously, 'they run to the Karens.'

It boggled the chairman's imagination that of all the ethnic groups, his people had invariably chosen to run to the Karens. Why not the Shans or some other ethnic group, he wondered. He felt quite insulted that his people saw in the Karens an indomitable protector, tough enough to deter his army from pursuing and punishing them.

'Yes, Chairman,' exclaimed General Khin Maung Nyunt. He hated the Karens who, with impunity, had constantly thwarted the attempts of the Tatmadaw to dislodge them from their strongholds. The humiliation of repeated failure with this ethnic group had grated his ego for, as the commander-in-chief of the army, he had failed to make good his obligation of success to the council.

'We should be receiving another shipment of arms now: grenade launchers, heavy mortars and some field artillery as well... 105s and 155s,' the chairman announced.

You may deploy these weapons with your men suitably around the camps of those dogs as soon as the rains get over,' he instructed.

'Yes, Chairman, I will make sure to do that,' accepted General Khin Maung Nyunt gratefully.

'And when the rascals cross into the Karen camps,' the chairman continued, 'order your men to blast the sons of bitches with everything they've got. Get the Karens, too. Let's wipe them out and their Kawthoolei!' he thundered, bringing his fist crashing down on the table with such force that a tumbler jumped involuntarily, spilling its contents on the draft of the plan. He looked at the commander-in-chief of the army and said, 'Send the Butcher. He's best suited for the job.'

The chairman and the generals had now thrown the dice and, with one throw, hoped to contain Aung San Suu Kyi's attempt to restore democracy and simultaneously exterminate their arch enemies, the Karens, once and for all. Before the generals left, the chairman issued a directive, saying, 'Those of you who will be involved in civilian affairs must get out of uniforms and wear civilian clothes when the new cabinet is formed. The new government must appear to have civilians as much as possible, at least in the beginning.'

'Good thinking, sir,' endorsed the council.

'That way, the common people will feel that the future will shift towards civilian rule eventually,' a general remarked.

The chairman had, however, refrained from disclosing another element to crown the plan for the time being. Once the coup was accomplished, he would advise the new cabinet to promise economic reforms and a new era of wealth and prosperity to the nation. There would be a liberalization of the economy. He had already decided on allowing foreign investors into the country. He would instruct the new regime to actively solicit foreign investments, set up collaborations and huge development projects in major sectors like oil and natural gas, mining for minerals, construction of roadways and any other that would make it lucrative for the greedy foreigners, so that a women's cry for democracy would sound inconvenient to them. He would look at Singapore, Japan, China, Korea and Australia. He would look at France. He would look at America. He would even look at India. Simultaneously, the new cabinet would also undertake a massive national reconciliation programme in the country…the scale of which, he was certain, would win over the monks, the scribes and the scholars, the educated and the illiterate, and with money coming their way, their political will. He envisaged the national programme attaining great popularity amongst the people, reducing Aung San Suu Kyi's movement to meaningless babble and an embarrassment, eventually a threat to their newly acquired well-being. That was when she would have been contained.

He gloated diabolically over the checkmate in his scheme to render the opposition impotent, and toyed with the idea of amassing a fortune for himself and his henchmen in the near future. He, of course, would bracket the best contracts and think of those hush-hush islands, and bathe regularly in dolphin blood, as he did earlier, to stay young and enjoy his wealth. He had four billion dollars with him already in a Swiss bank, and properties in Germany and Austria.

'Damn it,' cursed the chairman. His instincts had warned him that the fates of the Iranian Shah and the Marcos of the world could befall him in time, but had delayed that with all his might for as long as he could. Shaking off the fleeting premonition, he reassured himself with the thought that the Burmese were still a meek and gullible people. He glanced at the solemn face of Aung San, staring down at him accusingly from its golden frame hanging on the wall. The chairman shrugged his shoulders and turned his back on the mute photograph. The protégé had been independent of his mentor, and he would rid himself of the mentor's legacy as well if she pushed him to the wall.

Sanda Win

A Tea Shop in Rangoon
June 1988

The atmosphere in the city crackled with excitement, buzzing with gossip and the chatter of a new beginning in the country. U Tin Nu, who owned the little tea shop by the Shwedagon Pagoda, felt a surge of excitement coursing through his veins that morning as he opened his shop. Curious of the lively and fearless spirit that was dominant in the city—a mood he had not seen in Rangoon for a long time—he had passed by a meeting held by Aung San's daughter the previous night, and had felt the luminous charge sparkling in the crowd, infecting him.

The promise of change was intoxicating, but soon, as the morning advanced, he suppressed the swelling hope in him for fear of disappointment. The silence of the authorities had troubled him, for the twenty-six years of his experience of the Revolutionary Council and Burmese Socialist Party since 1962 told him that it was uncharacteristic. He was certain that the regime was planning a counter-strike, and feared that when it came it would be ugly and bloody.

'Good morning, sir,' greeted a group of youths and maidens, entering his shop for their morning tea, holding in their hands mounds of paper and rolls of cloth inscribed with paint, which U Tin Nu suspected to be banners. His worry that 'Sanda Win' was turning from an inconspicuous tea shop to a popular hub for dissident students was growing by the day, yet he had no resentment for them.

'Good morning, children,' he replied. 'Tea? Before you start your work for the day?'

'Yes, thank you, sir,' acknowledged the students. 'We have a very busy day today.'

'Oh. How come?' enquired the tea-shop owner.

'There's going to be a very big meeting, the biggest yet,' answered a student. 'Tomorrow.'

'Aung San Suu Kyi?' asked U Tin Nu.

'Yes,' came the enthusiastic reply. 'Have you been to one of the meetings?'

'Eh…eh….Yes, last night,' said U Tin Nu.

'Wasn't it good…? I mean, don't you believe in her?' asked a student with keen anticipation.

'Oh….I'm an old man now with a few more years to live,' replied U Tin Nu evasively, concealing his scepticism about the success of the movement. The youngsters sitting in his shop had a lot more to learn of their own government, he lamented.

'She has tremendous courage, sir,' stated a maiden.

'Yes….Yes…remarkable,' endorsed U Tin Nu. The courage of Aung San Suu Kyi had stupefied him, and he wondered how this diminutive woman expected to loosen the regime's grip on the nation.

'She's going to bring back democracy in our country,' asserted a youth.

'Have you had any clashes with soldiers?' enquired U Tin Nu after a pensive moment.

'No, but they're always there, always present, reminding us that we can't ignore them,' the maiden stated and laughed.

'Yes, yes…they are always,' U Tin Nu agreed with a chill. It was in this very tea shop that a few months ago, a student brawl over some audio tape being played led to the shooting and killing of one student by the heavily armed riot police. U Tin Nu was deeply aware of the growing resentment towards military rule, further exacerbated by economic mismanagement and corruption.

'I'm surprised they haven't moved on this one yet,' remarked U Tin Nu, meaning the movement.

'That's no surprise now,' answered a student. 'It's Aung San Suu Kyi, sir. That's the reason. They can't forget who her father was.'

'That is probably true,' agreed U Tin Nu and asked, pointing to the bundle of papers the students were carrying, 'What are those?'

'They're pamphlets for distribution, sir,' answered the maiden who had spoken earlier. 'They're messages of Aung San Suu Kyi to the people.'

'Oh, I see,' responded U Tin Nu.

'And these are banners, sir,' said a student proudly. 'See, we have our own party emblem now.' The student unfurled the banner excitedly for U Tin Nu, displaying a symbol. It was a peacock. Not the traditional bluish green of the graceful bird, but a red militant peacock entering a fray and ready for battle with the generals. The cry of the peacock, thought U Tin Nu, symbolized the cry for liberty taken up by a people awakened with this new hope, and captivated by the belief that the aura of Aung San would protect and deliver to his daughter their long-lost freedom.

'God go with you, my children,' he said as the group of students left the tea shop, and wondered whether her aura would protect them when she defied the generals of Rangoon to flashpoint.

'Will she do it?' he asked himself, cleaning the table the students had vacated, not certain that she would ultimately defy the army.

She did. Incredibly, she did.

Battle Cry

8 August–19 September 1988

The *Lon Htein*, Burma's armed riot police, had been overwhelmed by the numbers of protesters since late July. Beginning 1 August, the movement for the NLD gained momentum and as its following grew, the demonstrations in the streets of Rangoon became a focal point for other demonstrations beyond Rangoon. Activists in Rangoon contacted lawyers and citizens in Mandalay, encouraging them to take part in the protests. Burmese citizens from all walks of life—including government workers, Buddhist monks, air force and navy personnel, customs officers, teachers and hospital staff and even farmers—quickly joined the marches, swelling over a hundred thousand. About 10,000 protesters alone demonstrated outside the Sule Pagoda in Rangoon, where they buried effigies of Ne Win and the Butcher in coffins decorated with demonetized bank notes. 'Aung San Suu Kyi! Aung San Suu Kyi!' became the chant of the nation, and the chant of the people grew louder while the old prayed quietly in the privacy of their homes for liberation from a tyranny that had shackled and impoverished them for three decades and more.

The army promptly retaliated, promulgating martial law on 3 August. Elite Tatmadaw troops of the 22nd, 44th and 77th Light Infantry Divisions, who were well-experienced with counter-insurgency operations, were brought into Rangoon and deployed at strategic locations.

'Shoot the bastards!' the chairman thundered.

Just a little before midnight, the troops fired.

The soldiers who had been positioned earlier to cut off the escape of the demonstrators held their guns in readiness to discharge a greeting of death as soon as the fleeing mob surged onto their streets. The soldiers did not have to wait long, for soon the mob—no longer protected by the aura of Aung San or the immunity of his daughter—sought the safety of the narrow streets of Rangoon in the hope of evading the pursuing troops. The operation was planned in detail and the army was not intending to let its beloved mentor down. Students, the unwary public, the unfortunate pedestrians, the educated conscientious citizens, monks, young school children, boys and girls—and anyone that came in the way—were put down by gunfire. And when the shooting subsided, bodies, in their thousands, littered the streets of Rangoon—the body of U Tin Nu among one, lying in front of his tea shop in a pool of blood, his octogenarian head shattered and split open by an anonymous bullet, unburdened by a conscience or by guilt.

Beginning the day of 9 August, the streets downtown had been cleared but army troops kept on firing at demonstrators in the northern outskirts of Rangoon. The protesters had built barricades and, in retaliation, attacked police forces with pickaxes, sickles, knives, stones and stolen firearms, burning down several police stations and beheading six police officers.

On 10 August, a Tatmadaw battalion guided by Military Intelligence (MI) agents burst into the Rangoon General Hospital packed with hundreds of students, monks and demonstrators who had been wounded during the previous two days. Doctors and nurses tried to hang a banner at the entrance asking to stop the killings, but the soldiers shot at them with automatic weapons in cold blood, killing the doctors and the nurses, and dying civilians—not even sparing blood donors waiting to help outside the hospital. The MI agents were hunting down the leaders of the demonstrations since early August. The news of the incident spread like forest wildfire and, on that day, the army that Aung San had laboured to build, lost the little reverence the Burmese people still had for it.

The chairman of the erstwhile Revolutionary Council was disappointed that the much-hoped-for foreign involvement in the movement of Aung San's daughter had not surfaced, and the junta's effort to establish one had drawn a blank. He sat grimly in his chambers and reviewed the alarming report that the intelligence chief had submitted.

'The motherless curs!' swore the chairman, and snatched the telephone from its cradle, dialling Military Headquarters.

'Khin Maung Nyunt?' he demanded.

'Yes, Chairman?'

'Shoot the bastards!' he thundered. 'The miserable dogs are planning a demonstration in front of the American embassy.'

'In front of the embassy?' returned the incredulous voice on the telephone.

'Shoot them anywhere, I don't care….No, I don't care for the Americans, damn it! This is our country.'

'Won't we be drawing attention to ourselves, Chairman?' replied the voice urging caution. 'Maybe she wants it to happen that way.'

'Okay. Herd them away from the embassy and then shoot them on the Maha Bundula Street or Anawratha Street. Coordinate with Myo Mint. Shoot the whole bloody lot.'

'And her?' asked the voice apprehensively, seeking clarification.

'No, damn it! Not her….I personally doubt that she will be there….The woman's as cunning as a fox.'

'And if she's there?' came the voice again, irritating the chairman abundantly.

'Uhh? Put her under house arrest or something like that, you idiot!' he yelled. The chairman was dismayed that no one was willing to take personal responsibility when it came to the direct question of Aung San's daughter.

'Very well, Chairman,' replied the voice. 'It will be done.'

'And one more thing, Khin Maung Nyunt,' said the chairman.

'Yes, Chairman?' asked the voice obediently on the phone.

'Any soldier that does not obey the command will be transferred to the south; they can fight the Karens. Tell them that,' he barked and slammed the phone down.

The chairman had been alarmed when he heard that some of the troops had refused to open fire on an earlier occasion, and had to be confined to their barracks. He had no time for the re-education of these troops now, he fumed. He'd let them die fighting the Karens instead and save himself the bother, he swore, and then dialled for the man in charge of the Ministry of Information and Broadcast.

'Complete news blackout, make sure of that,' he ordered into the telephone as soon as the Information and Broadcast man came on line. 'Deny everything, you hear? Khin Maung Nyunt's men will be having some target practice soon.'

'Yes, sir,' answered a meek voice on the telephone.

Running from automatic gunfire, demonstrators had run towards the American and Indian embassies on Merchant Street, next to the Maha Bundula Gardens.

The SLORC

The American Embassy
Rangoon

Ryan sipped his coffee before he took the guard. He had heard gunfire a few moments ago and was convinced of another tense day in Rangoon. He counted the days left before he flew out of the city to the Philippines for his vacation. He was sickened and terrified by the recent events in the city, and had hoped to get away from the calamity at the earliest. Most embassies, including his own, were flying out staff and citizens from the country, fearing another bloodbath. He now foreboded a prelude to an even bloodier confrontation between the conflicting forces in the country.

'Good morning, sir,' he greeted and saluted Undersecretary Mark Stevens who walked into the embassy. The marine sergeant then took up command of the guard at the gates of the embassy.

'Sarge!' shouted a guard at him an hour later, pointing northwards of the embassy. 'Do you see what I see?'

'They're military trucks, aren't they?' Sergeant Ryan queried as he squinted in the glare of the sun. He counted a convoy of 10 army trucks.

'Yup,' acknowledged the guard.

'Hey, what's that?' shouted another guard, pointing southwards. 'Some kind of pilgrimage to the Sule?'

'Jesus Christ! I'll be damned!' exclaimed Sergeant Ryan. 'That's no pilgrimage; that's the Lady Suu Kyi's party!' The sergeant had recognized the red and orange banners, and the unmistakable symbol of the surging peacock.

'Heck, I reckon there's going to be some kind of scrap with soldier boys yonder there, and they're sure as hell coming this way,' the first guard said.

'Alright guys, whatever it is, it spells trouble,' Sergeant Ryan decided. 'Get in now and lock the gates pronto while I go brief Mr Stevens.'

The sergeant rushed to the flight of stairs in the embassy while his men below hurriedly closed the gates, edgy now at the distinct chant of the crowd approaching the embassy. The army trucks had screeched to a halt in front of the embassy, cordoning the premises of the building when Sergeant Ryan barged into Undersecretary Stevens' office. Stevens had heard the screech of tyres and the audible chant of the demonstrators.

'Aung San Suu Kyi! Aung San Suu Kyi!' the chant growing louder and louder as the crowd ran to the embassy.

'Trouble, I suppose,' Stevens remarked. 'Somehow it's always us they choose. Why not the others, I wonder?'

'Poor sods!' Sergeant Ryan hissed under his breath as he saw the commotion of streaming bodies, followed by the soldiers who began shooting.

'They're doing it!' exclaimed Undersecretary Stevens, recoiling in horror as the crash of rifle fire struck a resonant chord with the screams of the demonstrators.

'This is a massacre,' Stevens said. 'I'd better make my report.'

'Gosh!' exclaimed the sergeant, transfixed by the steady reports of rifle fire. 'How can they do this to their own people?'

'They've done it before, time and again, Sergeant,' observed Stevens. 'Slaughter is nothing new to them.'

Burton Levin, the US ambassador, saw army troops on rooftops picking off students and shooting those fleeing, and was stunned when an American diplomat was shot at while driving through the commotion.

'By God, they're being picked off like rabbits!' he exclaimed.

The diplomat survived. The United States diplomatic staff helped students and political activists who managed to get through the embassy gates.

Elsewhere on Merchant Street, the Indian ambassador, Dr I.P. Singh, organized an emergency hospital in the library of the embassy.

A British military attaché was hit with rifle butts in the middle of Strand Street.

In a rare diplomatic condemnation, the Japanese ambassador, Ohtaka Hiroshi, asked the authorities to stop the crackdown on civilians after the first news of the shootings broke out.

On the 12th, the Butcher resigned on grounds of ill health.

The 13th left many protestors confused but jubilant that the Butcher was no longer in power. But the Tatmadaw still made its presence felt, exercising caution now with demonstrators, particularly in neighbourhoods totally under the control of the demonstrators. On the 19th, pressure to form a civilian government led to the appointment of Dr Maung Maung as head of government. Ne Win's biographer and a legal scholar, he was the only non-military entity to serve in the Burma Socialist Programme Party. The appointment briefly resulted in a lull.

However, demonstrations resumed on the 22nd. About 1,00,000 people—including Buddhist monks—protested in Mandalay. About 50,000 demonstrated in Sittwe. Large marches took place from Taunggyi and Moulmein to distant ethnic states, where brutal military campaigns were conducted. Two days later, doctors, monks, musicians, actors, lawyers, army veterans and government office workers joined the protests.

On the 26th, Aung San Suu Kyi addressed half a million people at the Shwedagon Pagoda. It was at this point that she became a symbol of struggle in the eyes of the Western world.

Ne Win waited.

*

Phase one of the plan had been implemented. It was time now for the second phase of the plan to be put in motion.

The Burmese Socialist Program Party announced they would be organizing an election, but the opposition parties called for the immediate resignation of the party from government. They also rejected U Maung Maung, and demanded an interim government to organize elections.

Ne Win rejected both demands.

Protesters again took to the streets on 12 September as expected by him. Aung San Suu Kyi's movement had relied on three expectations. First, daily demonstrations to coerce the regime to yield to their demands; second, encouraging soldiers to defect; and third, emoting an appeal to an international audience that awoke in August, with the hope that United Nations or United States troops would arrive to arbiter. By mid-September, the protests grew more violent and lawless.

Ne Win struck. As designed by the Burmese Machiavelli, his police and army began fraternizing with the protesters in the movement. Soon, the imbedded soldiers deliberately led protesters into skirmishes which his army won.

On 18 September 1988, the Tatmadaw retook power in the country and established the State Law and Order Restoration Council (SLORC), imposing more draconian measures than Ne Win had imposed. Of the 21 members of the council, not even one was a civilian. The SLORC imposed martial law and protests were violently broken up. Tatmadaw troops went through cities throughout Burma, indiscriminately firing on protestors. It is estimated that within the first week of securing power, 1,000 students, monks and schoolchildren were killed, and another 500 were killed whilst protesting outside the United States Embassy—recorded by a cameraman nearby who distributed the footage to the world's media. Protestors were also pursued into the jungle, and some students took up training on the country's borders with Thailand.

*

Yangon
January 1989

Aung San Suu Kyi's mother had died on 27 December 1988. Throngs of supporters had showed up at the funeral. She criticized the brutality of the government and demanded democratic reforms. The generals realized that here was no longer a bud they could nip. The lotus had reached full bloom. Her meetings became more frequent and more provocative. She was displaying her mettle to the generals. During a meeting on 5th April, she was placed in front of a firing squad, but just before they were going to shoot, a senior officer stopped them. She was given the choice of staying in Burma under house arrest or leave and enjoy her freedom, never to return to the country.

Aung San Suu Kyi stayed.

The regime did the next predictable thing. Aung San Suu Kyi was placed under house arrest in July 1989. The witch-hunt then commenced on schedule. *The New Light of Myanmar*, the state owned-paper, began splashing smear campaigns on the NLD, questioning the integrity of her followers and the leader of the movement. The intelligence arm resorted to untraceable acts of violence. Some members of the movement disappeared.

Aung Gyi and Tin Oo found themselves in jail again with other leaders of the movement with harsh sentences, and the chase of the dissidents began. The oracle of the erstwhile chairman had been above reproach; the dissidents and the students were heading for the Karen camps.

Kawthoolei!

*

India, 1990

The events in Yangon had interested the Karens as well—those in the jungles and those out of the country. The guerrillas on the southern hill tracks of the country thought their camps might get a needy respite from the attentions of the Burmese Army while it lavished its heat on the movement of Aung San Suu Kyi, allowing them a chance to repair the damage caused by the intermittent Burmese shelling. Unlike the guerrillas in Myanmar, the Karens abroad thought it possible that they might be able to visit relatives and set foot once again on the soil where they were born.

'Simon, I'd like to visit Burma and stay there for a while,' Dora expressed her wish.

'You won't get beyond the airport, Mom, even if you're allowed to land,' replied Simon.

He had been following the reports keenly and often thought about the other branch of his relatives in Burma, and had always wondered how they were getting on. Communication had ceased and Simon accepted that relationships tended to lose their lustre when time stepped in, and so, he distanced them over 20 years and more. They, too, would be struggling for a livelihood in an invidious environment like he was—with the exception that while his was just economic, theirs was political as well, and probably harder, since most of them would have returned to their villages.

'Why? It'll be a while only before Aung San Suu Kyi forms a democratic government in Burma,' she countered.

'Aung San Suu Kyi is the best thing that's happened in Burma since the death of her father, Mom, but do you think the generals will give in easily?' he asked mildly. 'Don't forget that they've placed her under house arrest already.'

'The army might revolt,' she offered. 'After all, she is the daughter of Aung San, the father of the army.'

'That,' he concurred, 'is an interesting angle; the younger fellows who have not yet prospered. Hmm…but they, too, would need a leader amongst them to stir them into action.'

'Aung San Suu Kyi might be able to persuade their conscience if she can get to them, but I don't know how she'd get anywhere near their barracks. The generals won't allow it.'

Simon pursued the opportunity of his mother accepting the futility of dreams of returning to Burma.

'Mom, you've heard of that old saying—"Old wine in new bottle"—haven't you? It's the same gang with a different label. They're not even using a new bottle; they don't have one. It's the old man Ne Win still pulling strings behind the curtain and his puppets have nowhere to go,' he commented.

This was not the French or the American Revolution, nor did Aung San Suu Kyi have suicidal firebrands like Che Guevara, Simon introspected. It was apparent to him that in order to disable the regime, a nationwide upheaval was called for; an upheaval where the armed forces, the police, the ecclesiasts and the academicians were in consonance with its people—including the ethnic groups. It was the only way in which Aung San Suu Kyi could affect a change in the country and reconstitute a government. And that process, Simon realized sadly, demanded more blood because the regime was past reason.

What she seemed to have, thought Simon, was her own incredible courage, a very frightened populace, several thousand educated brave people who bore no arms, and a sense of unrelatedness with the ethnic peoples that was any match to the guns of the generals. And if she pushed the generals any further, Simon was certain that they would claw back with the ferocity of a trapped, desperate animal. Possibly foreboding danger to her life, he feared.

*

27 May 1990

To Simon's surprise, the generals finally called for elections with the confidence that Aung San Suu Kyi's following would have been intimidated, and her party would be leaderless as she bravely bore the isolation of house arrest. Amazingly, the gamble of the generals backfired! Aung San Suu Kyi and the NLD won a resounding victory in the elections, carrying the verdict of a people to the military regime. The game was over for the generals, or so she and her party thought in their premature and short-lived joy. Their backs to the wall now, the stunned SLORC did the only thing they could do. They ignobly reneged on their promise to the people and annulled the election' results, and extended Aung San Suu Kyi's house arrest.

The voice of national consensus was ingloriously castigated and denied its constitutional rights to government. In Yangon, a curtain had descended upon Aung San Suu Kyi—a curtain lacquered with the guilt of the generals, the impotence of a people and the wantonness of a young, uncivilized army.

Solomon's Hill

The Karen Camps
Myanmar
1990–1995

In the early somnolence of the dawn, the village on the hill looked quiet and pristine—its huts blending with the milieu, and at peace with the mist that was still in the air. Desultory spirals of smoke twirled hazily upwards from some of the thatched roofs, communing discreetly with the dew, suggesting that there were early risers in the community preparing the first meal of the day.

Palm and banana groves swayed in verdant grace, delicately dancing with the gentle breeze that was humming around the village, welcoming a spell of dry sunshine while the dense teaks kept their vigil for a familiar intruder.The vigil was not in vain. The teak trees—tall and formidable in their knowledge of the matters of men—knew that with the end of the rains, the expected offensive of the Burmese Army would be here.

General Sein Lwin scrutinized the village with his impassive binoculars. The high-powered lens scoured the ground around the village, leaving to the pair of aggressive eyes of the general the vexing task of determining a path his troops would take for the assault. The irked general found none except a narrow gorge that led to the village. As a military commander, he knew the implications of an uphill assault, and had never favoured the odds against his troops in such a situation—especially when the foe was a battle-hardened body of the tenacious Karens.

He didn't consider the Burmese students sheltering in the village undergoing training in warfare of any consequence, but fretted instead about the guerrillas and their field of fire. Of the withering fire that would descend upon his troops, he had no doubt. A fire fight had to be expected, but his chief concern was the gorge that would lead him to the hill. The docile appearance of the torpid hill on which the village hibernated in slumber did not deceive him. This was Hill 4044, the gateway to Manerplaw—a sprawling base where thousands of fleeing Karen civilians were sheltered. It was also the political headquarters of the Karen National Union. The fall of the hill would spell the doom of the Karens, for it would throw Manerplaw wide open to capture by the Burmese Army; an irresistible target that presented opportunities to an ambitious army. The general's wistful mind returned to his present distasteful task.

The gorge.

'Mines!' he thought aloud. There would be mines. He couldn't risk a probe for that would alert the village on the hill, he reasoned, and consoled himself with the card up his sleeve.

Surprise!

He thought of the village itself. It, in fact, was a well-fortified camp with trenches and bunkers lined with strong teak on their seams and roofs. The bunkers were buffeted further with sandbags and caked mud of the rains. Camouflaged with stems and leaves from the palm and banana by the grateful Burmese students and an industrious team of Karen women and children of the camp, it was one of the last bastions of defence left for the Karens.

Most identified camps had fallen one after another, their survivors fleeing to Thailand, just across the Moei River, to become refugees or dissolve into the remote density of the jungle beyond the immediate reach of the Burmese Army. General Sein Lwin considered the political implications of the successful outcome of this battle, and knew how important it was to the generals in Yangon that the village be taken. This was a command he hadn't wanted, a command that was thrust upon him and an order he couldn't refute. He was a dead man either way, he thought cynically, and cursed the day he had decided to become a soldier.

General Sein Lwin promptly put aside his infamous past in Rangoon and the personal unease that some knew him as the Butcher, and summoned his leading officers to deliver his pre-battle exhortation. 'Officers of the Tatmadaw,' he said in a hoarse whisper, fearing that the teak had ears and would steal from him his advantage of surprise.

'This is the last enemy camp to stand in our way, and I don't have to remind you of the importance of its capture.

'With this camp removed, nothing will stand in our way to Manerplaw. It will be ready for the plucking. The Karens, as an army, will not have any more tangible presence on our soil after that. They'll have to scatter onto the hills, making it easy for us to take them piecemeal at our leisure, or they will have to withdraw deep into the jungle where they will perish from starvation and disease. I'm not quite sure they will survive as guests of the Thai government when the Thais see the new military of our country.

'It is for the glory of Myanmar, your fathers and mothers, your sweethearts, your wives and children that this camp is to be destroyed.

'So, no matter what the cost, you cannot fail when your other comrades have succeeded elsewhere,' summed up the general, reminding his officers of the recent successes the Burmese Army have had against the Karens.

The officers nodded in quiet unison. Morale was high and confident of a victory, they were prepared to lead their men.

They were not to know, however, that the teak jungle that hid them had already sent whispers of warning of the impending attack to the village.

'Get your men into position,' he ordered his officers. 'We will commence attack in one hour.'

General Sein Lwin's officers moved agilely, deploying their troops at the tree line and bringing up the artillery: mortars, grenade launchers and the howitzers that they had lugged across for the attack. The army was well-armed as never before against this astute enemy, and was sanguine that this time the enemy would taste a bit of their own medicine. The soldiers of the Tatmadaw felt invincible.

*

Commander Solomon eyed his lieutenants while sipping a cup of plain tea, and cogitated upon the information his scouts had brought.

'How many?' he enquired again, hoping that he had heard it wrong.

'Hundreds of them, perhaps thousands,' estimated one of the scouts agitatedly. This was by far the largest body of Burmese troops to ever approach the Karens for battle in a decade.

'This must be a combined force,' conjectured another scout, informed of the simultaneous attacks that had taken place on different camps a few days ago. 'But how did they get here? So many of them?' questioned one of his aides. 'We would have known about it.'

'I'll tell you how. It's the Buddhist faction that must have shown them the way,' a lieutenant offered in explanation. 'They know the jungle tracks as well as we do.'

'They're Karens, damn it!' exclaimed a guerrilla.

Commander Solomon raised his hand, and the gesture stilled the command bunker immediately.

'It doesn't matter now whether they're Karens, Christians or Buddhists or who brought the Burmese here,' he said, looking at his men. 'It's an army out there and they plan to annihilate us. We have a big fight coming our way now.'

Years of fighting had eroded the spirit of his people, diluting the commitment to their cause and bringing to the surface their individual differences. Intrigue, insolence and intransigence had culminated in an ugly factionalism that had disintegrated the Karen National Army (KNA) as a cogent force, a force the Burmese Army had never got the better of in half a century. He didn't mind those who left, tired of the fighting and just wanting to live a peaceful and normal life with their families across the border, but was aggrieved with the faction that had aligned themselves with the Burmese authorities. Was it just the issue of religion, or a perceived political advantage that could be attained in the future, or was it just greed for power that knifed through a common bond and prompted the faction that was now conniving with the enemy and leading the Burmese Army to this camp? Solomon no longer cared. He cared only about the camp, and the enemy hidden in the tree line that was going to obliterate it along with its women and children.

'We have less than 300, not counting the students. I hope by now they have learnt to shoot; it's their war as well,' declared a lieutenant in a tone of finality. Some of the fugitives had their own volition, and had voiced their desire to fight the army.

Commander Solomon shook his head.

'Don't count on them now. This is not a drill but the real thing,' he cautioned his men.

Commander Solomon was a realist and had some scruples about involving the students in a fire fight. He personally foresaw only confusion amongst the students when the shooting started; a confusion that would prove a handicap and diffuse the focus he needed in his men. He could do without the confusion. Besides, he considered, he needed to conserve his ammunition.

'Send the women and children across now,' he ordered a scout and grasped a twig lying by his feet. He hastily delineated on the ground his defences, and positioned the twig where the narrow gorge was.

'They'll have to come up here,' he stated without hesitation. 'The path's mined and we have the machine guns in position. Bring up the mortars here,' he said pointing to a spot on his makeshift map.

'Shoot only when I give the order,' he continued. 'They will start with a barrage any time now.'

He knew what to expect, now that the enemy possessed artillery. Of late, the Burmese Army was increasingly deploying artillery and the calibre was getting heavier, he noted with unhappiness.

'I want everyone down in the bunkers and when the barrage ceases, the men on our flanks should be alert just in case they try flanking us…but that will be difficult for them. Nevertheless, let's not exclude the possibility. Their morale has improved since their recent victories.'

'I'll be here,' he said, positioning himself at the mouth of the gorge.

Commander Solomon's lieutenants hurried about their tasks swiftly, and in less than half an hour had positioned their defence according to plan. The men displayed remarkable courage; an attestation to their battle-readiness and to their skill in repelling superior forces over innumerable encounters. He was satisfied that they would give a good account of themselves in the coming clash as they had always done in the past. Their spirit had not sagged, despite the knowledge that they would be killing some of their kind.

They had trained well, Commander Solomon observed, and was proud of their discipline. This was not the flamboyant KNDO of the old, he mused. No dilettantes like the sea princes and arrogant generals like Alexander, but just simple men with a votive dedication to preserve the heritage of their people.

They were also educated like him, and had been driven to this out of frustration: teachers, civil servants, university students, musicians, artisans and Bible scholars. They even had a veterinarian in the camp! But they were now unfortunate veterans of a gun culture with one consuming passion: to live their birth right as Karens, Solomon believed. He was also gratified that there were others, too, who recognized their right to liberty, equality and justice.

He missed Guillaume now, the red-haired Frenchman who had become a legend amongst them. The Frenchman had sympathized with their plight and had fought fiercely along with them until a Burmese sniper's bullet had prematurely inscribed his epitaph. He had terrorized the Burmese troops for a short while before paying the final price with his life for his belief, Solomon recollected with a saddened heart. He wished there were more like the Frenchman in the world who would accord the Karens their rights as human beings.

Commander Solomon surveyed his position meticulously. He had the river to his back, and beyond the river was Thailand. He was indebted to the Thais; but for them, his people and the Burmese fugitives would have perished a long time ago. Here, on Burmese territory, he had the gorge in front of him and steep slopes on his flanks, a hard and discouraging climb for the soldiers in the trees. The thought evoked a smile in Solomon.

He held the high ground.

Sein Lwin's Salvoes

'Fire!' General Sein Lwin barked.

The Burmese artillery thundered their salvoes of death upon the village. The barrage was intense. The heat from the flashing guns parched the air and singed the leaves of the teak, putting to flight irate wings that had nested the night on the boughs of the trees. The teak swooned in despair and the foliage ran riot, loveless, while the guns roared in a carnival of smoke and lightning. A while longer, thought an ebullient General Sein Lwin, before the village was pulverized, and that was when he would send his troops in.

'Send the troops in now,' he ordered an hour later. His casualty would be less, the general estimated hopefully, but still worried about the mines.

The first wave went in, the adrenaline pumping in the soldiers as they charged up the gorge, shouting their battle cry, but in a flash, the earth heaved under and around them, and devoured them whole along with their officers.

The second wave had not realized what had happened and didn't know what was in store for them as they joined their comrades in the dominion of death. Charging through the dust and flying mounds of earth, the third wave was mowed down by concerted motor and machine-gun fire.

It was then that General Sein Lwin realized that something was terribly wrong. It wasn't just the mines.

The Karens were firmly entrenched and were better-armed than he had assumed....But above all, they were waiting for him!

The realization subdued him with shock. By the time he pulled himself together, the fourth wave had realized what they were up against, and were rolling back in confusion and defeat.

'Call off the attack! Call off the attack!' General Sein Lwin bellowed and his remaining officers relayed orders like automatons, themselves confounded by the rapid deterioration of the attack.

*

Back on the Hill

The fusillade from the Burmese artillery had abated, and the advancing tide of soldiers had faltered to a straggle. Dust and cordite fumes were clearing with the wind while Solomon assessed the damage his camp had sustained. Many bunkers had caved in, hit by multiple salvoes; the teak reinforcements were reduced now to burning cinders—a pyre on which the mangled, broken dead lay. Apart from that, there were some injured by splinters and flying debris. Some of them would fight yet, while some would have to be evacuated across the river, where they would receive medical attention from the Red Cross.

God bless the Red Cross, he thanked gratefully.

He darted along the perimeter of his defences, keeping himself low, wary of a sharp shooter's lucky bullet. He ensured that his men were in position on the flanks to shoot down at any of the soldiers who might hazard the arduous climb. He then summoned his lieutenants to the command bunker for a situation appraisal.

'They will take a while regrouping,' he said, 'but they will be back soon.'

'The mines are gone, they'll know,' said a lieutenant, grinning with satisfaction over the surprise the charging troops must have felt.

'We have to move around our mortars,' advised another.

'They will try to knock them out next time, I know,' Commander Solomon agreed, nodding his head.

'Move them around the camp; they're light, but make sure of the trajectory,' he insisted. 'The mouth of the gorge has to be ranged in. We must not let them get into the village.'

'What about the students?' enquired one of his men.

'There are some who want to fight, Solomon,' reminded an aide.

'Maybe we can use them as reserves,' proposed another. Commander Solomon then remembered the students in the village. He had been preoccupied by the next onslaught that was expected. He thought over the question for a few minutes and debated in his mind on the wisdom of arming them. He appreciated the fact that he needed every available fighting man now, especially in view of the legion hiding in the teak, but he had a larger consideration on his mind.

'No,' he said at last. 'Get them across the border now, and let them take the wounded with them.'

'Why?' asked one of his aides, more curious than resentful of Solomon's decision.

'Because,' Commander Solomon answered, 'they're just students, untrained and undisciplined for this kind of fight…and are bound to get in our way should the fight reach us here.'

'Quite right,' agreed a lieutenant.

'Besides,' Solomon continued, pausing for a moment before he disclosed his paramount reason, 'they are Burmese and we are Karens; they are citizens and we're rebels, right? The truth is that simple.'

'They're no more citizens now than we are,' commented a lieutenant.

'I'll accept that,' interposed Solomon, exhaling slowly before he tried to explain his view on the matter to his lieutenants. 'The problem they have with their government is a Burmese problem and that problem has to be solved by them. They're demanding democracy for their society, while our demand is for independent statehood. Besides, we have not been invited to join their cause and I can understand why; these are two different issues that cannot be mixed now. It would be bad politics for their leadership.'

Commander Solomon waited for a response from his men and, receiving none, was satisfied that his men were keenly following his argument.

'We are fighting for our rights to Karen independence in this country, and the fight is with the Burmese government. Our fight will continue until we have achieved an accord, whether with this government or the next.'

'But won't democracy be a wonderful thing for everyone?' asked a lieutenant.

'I'm certain it will be,' answered Solomon. 'But let us not confuse the issues involved here. Although we migrated to this land across the Gobi desert—which our legends refer to as the River of Sand—more than 4,000 years ago, we still don't have a homeland. They, the Burmese, moved in later and what did they do? They grabbed the country. The animosity between our peoples go back hundreds of years, and is still evident in modern times. We know full well what the attitude of the present government and of the previous one has been to our people.

'What we don't want is a future government of theirs to think of us as convenient partisans to be opportunely used and discarded once they have achieved their objectives.'

'Yes, just like the British had done to us,' commented an elderly guerrilla.

Commander Solomon had elucidated his concern for the political future of his people, and his men were beginning to comprehend the depth in meaning of what he had stated.

'So our message to the Burmese and their governments, this or another, will always be the same. We cannot be kept away from national politics anymore. We are not a seditious people, nor are we like Khun Sa, the Shan and this army. We are not drug barons fighting for poppy fields. We are just a people who want recognition of a Karen state, not a country, mind you, where our people can live their lives in peace and preserve their heritage,' Solomon concluded.

The guerrillas had no quarrel with their commander on his emphasis for the need to emerge from the conflict in the country as an independent entity with rights to their existence; they had taken to arms for that very purpose. They discerned the wisdom of their commander in advising them against the danger of subverting or diluting their perspective.

'We've had a breed of irresponsible and inconsiderate individuals in the movement, whose cynical heroics have tarnished our cause and distorted our tradition of generosity and kindness with their thirst for blood,' reminded Solomon to his men.

'But that is the past. Today, we are a different breed of men, better educated and sensitive to our need of a future. Our people require a capable generation to espouse their needs and we are that generation. Ours is the responsibility, and we will die if we have to, to achieve for them their dreams,' he entreated his men.

The men were quiet for a while, each empathetic of the pain and hope in Solomon of a future for a people in which they wouldn't need guns to preserve their identities. Commander Solomon then returned to the subject of the fugitives in his camp.

'We will shelter those who come to us, regardless of who they are. We will feed them and protect them and ease their pain if possible, but we will not arm them here because this fight is ours,' he asserted.

Commander Solomon had spoken his mind and he hoped that his concern for the students would perceive the extent of his concern for the bigger picture. The students were merely a transient element in this conflict, while their struggle would probably be ongoing until a solution was found, and that initiative lay with the Burmese, if not with the world.

'Do you think Aung San Suu Kyi will succeed?' asked a lieutenant.

There was a keen interest amongst the guerrillas in the appearance of Aung San Suu Kyi on the national political stage. They had followed with admiration her progress in defiance of the military government, and had almost considered her cause as victorious when she won the elections—until the generals in Rangoon had declared it void. They were surprised, however, when she was placed under house arrest; they had expected worse.

'She's been given the Nobel Prize already, don't forget,' Solomon answered and continued, 'it gives a signal to the present regime.' He had been relieved at the concern expressed by the world community.

'Yes, she should, if the world bodies and the media accelerate their censure of the present regime. And I pray that they do before the bastards in Rangoon think of a way of doing away with her,' a lieutenant voiced his personal apprehension.

'Yes. She's our only hope!' declared another.

'Yes, she is,' Commander Solomon agreed, and said so with conviction to his men. 'As the daughter of Aung San, I expect that she will honour her father's promises to our people.'

He knew that the cause of the Karens was of little significance, and didn't quite merit attention in the international spectrum of politics compared to the stature her call for democracy would achieve in the eyes of the world. And if the NLD came to power, the Karens could hope for a fair and reasonable hearing at the table. But the Karens needed her respect for that, and the only way he could think of earning that was to get the students to safety across the river. These were the people who, when she came to power, would play a role in the reconstruction of the nation…and he hoped they wouldn't forget the Karens who had provided them with sanctuary.

His train of thoughts was rudely interrupted when a salvo crashed into the village. The second attack was on, he surmised.

'Get the students out now,' he shouted above the din of the explosions, 'and everyone to their bunkers.'

The melee among the students was apparent as they rushed to the river, some crowding onto the bamboo rafts while some braving the swift current with bare feet, seeking the shallow depths of the muddy waters. Several shells fell amongst them, exploding and tasting blood, chastising them for their errant ways. They, too, would have to pay their price. Salvo after salvo exploded in the village while Solomon and his men prepared for the next assault.

*

Two hours into the attack had cost General Sein Lwin 300 dead and injured. The general's chagrin at the appalling decimation of his troops presently found its relief in the bark of the artillery, now firing and venting his rancour upon the village that had dared to tatter the morale of his army. He swore he would exterminate this camp, and called his officers for a conference to revise his battle plan.

'Fellow officers,' he raged, 'I know it will be hard but we must flank them, and very quickly at that. We can't keep sending our men through that gorge!'

'Yes, sir,' concurred a major, 'they're heavily concentrated on top there.'

All his officers nodded in a daze.

'We will keep pounding them to keep them down while a body of our troops moves out to the right and scale the hill. Do it silently,' the brigadier ordered.

'When you've secured your position, radio back. Then we'll move a body up that blasted gorge and synchronize our attack,' General Sein Lwin spat out his strategy vehemently, and nominated the officer who would lead the flanking troops.

'With attack from two sides, we should be able to dislodge them from their positions quickly. No prisoners. Is that understood?'

General Sein Lwin had laid down his rule of combat; he was now thinking of genocide.

'They're bound to have men on their flanks, sir,' advised a junior officer.

'I don't doubt that,' resorted the beleaguered general, scowling with rebuke at the hesitant officer. 'Just execute the order. And for God's sake, be soldiers, not women!'

The bellicose general was thinking of a far more dangerous consequence that would befall him if he failed to take the camp. How would he explain the failure to the chairman—the supremo who sat in the safe confines of his home in Yangon?

General Sein Lwin watched the troops move out for their perilous climb to flank the Karens, while some took up position for the charge of the gorge. It was noon already and the atmosphere was incandescent with urgency, for he would have a few hours of sunlight left to exact some measure of retribution, he thought ravenously.

Several huts had caught fire around the village, burning down and reducing themselves to crackling embers. An evanescent veil of smoke and dust was smouldering and disappearing with the breeze, only to appear in another place, like apparitions of giant butterflies in search of nectar among the dead in the village, thought Solomon.

An hour and a half later, Commander Solomon's men, embedded on the slopes of the hillside, noticed the rustle of leaves and heard the faint snap of twigs in the thick foliage advancing towards them from below. They sent word to Solomon.

The salvoes from the artillery had been falling at an even interval on the village, and the guerrillas, keeping track of the intervals between the salvoes, had been busy scurrying from bunker to bunker and shifting their mortars and machine guns. They couldn't estimate the strength of the force moving up the hill, but knew that the Burmese wouldn't venture a small body. This had to be the flanking movement Solomon had taken into account earlier in laying out his strategy for the defence of the village.

'Open up the mortars within a hundred metres of their approach,' advised Commander Solomon. That, he calculated, would compel the advancing force to break their crouch and expose their positions—just the kind of vulnerability his machine gunners could exploit with excruciating effect.

'Aim your machine guns low and use your grenades if they get any closer,' he ordered, and signalled his gunners at the mouth of the gorge to be alert for the expected rush of the enemy. He was rather surprised that the enemy was considering a two-pronged attack instead of their usual human wave tactic, and grudgingly admitted his respect for the Burmese commander. It also told him that the enemy wanted his hill dearly.

The gunners on the flank opened fire with their mortars and machine guns suddenly, when the cautiously creeping and advancing jungle had reached the hundred metres, catching the soldiers in complete unpreparedness, and cutting them down low like a monstrous scythe shearing undesirable weed.

'Attack...! Ah....Ah. Under attac....' a garbled radio message escaped the lips of a dying officer, and in the confusion, the order to charge up the gorge was given. General Sein Lwin had just committed the lives of a hundred men to the waiting guns of Commander Solomon. The Burmese Army was to learn that fighting in the paddy was not training enough to catch this enemy unawares.

A regal sun was setting in the western sky, glimpsing briefly at the Burma–Thai border and the teak that surrounded the village, helpless at the drama that was ending for the day. Men had fought for their prejudices and ideologies, shedding blood and shattering bone throughout its cosmic ascent during the day. It felt a moment of respite from the carnage below, before it bid the horizon farewell, but only for a moment. It knew, with a sense of futility, that when it visited this sky again in the morning, the men below would resume the bloodbath aggressively as the day before.

*

General Sein Lwin, seething with frustration, ordered his troops to regroup again and, as they began to tend their wounded and cook the first meal of the day, he gathered his officers and pondered upon a way to salvage the military disaster of his Tatmadaw. The generals in Rangoon would be unforgiving, he feared, but despite the staggering casualty, there would be a reprieve if they did take the Karen camp. Of that he was sure.

'We can't wait until their ammunition gets exhausted,' he lamented. 'We've got to find a way.'

'What about the air force, sir?' asked an officer. 'Surely they can strafe the camp.'

'They won't send the planes. They're far too precious,' the general stated sarcastically. He knew that the country's fledgling air force was unwilling to risk its planes to enemy fire ever since they lost a few of them during earlier operations.

'I'll try anyway.'

This was the army's fight and the events of the day had distanced him from the prospect of a quick victory, the general thought bitterly. His causalities had been preposterous. Damn those Karens, he cursed and recoiled at the imminent disgrace that would certainly cripple what was left of his career should the Karens succeed in repelling his forces any further. He urged his men to focus on a victory that he sorely needed now. His wrath had dissolved into self-pity, and was nearing a state of sulking when an officer suggested deploying all their troops in one thrust and overwhelming them with numbers. 'And lose half of them in one go?' demanded the general. 'Talk some sense, man!'

'Even if we do it, the dogs could run across the river,' commented another officer disdainfully.

'That would be a pity because our dead wouldn't be avenged,' observed one bitterly.

'I wish we could get in from behind and attack,' thought an officer out loud.

'What?' General Sein Lwin's ears pricked with alertness on hearing the officer. An alternative to a frontal assault sounded appealing to him, but thought he had examined the possibility earlier.

'Fetch me the map,' he ordered and reached for his torch, wondering whether he had overlooked an inconspicuous feature on the map, and began to hope for a track besides the river that could lead his men to the rear of the camp. One just had to look for it, he said to himself, attempting to convince himself that he would discover one.

A thin sharp beam roved the map as his finger coursed along its geographical contours, eagerly searching for a physical feature that he may have missed or had not considered. He was looking at Thailand beyond the Karen camp.

'Behind the camp is the river. It's Thai territory,' observed an officer unwittingly.

'I know that, you idiot! But who's to tell? The river flows through our territory as well,' snarled General Sein Lwin in vexation, while his mind raced the contours of the map, probing for an answer. There was none on his side of the border. Think! He demanded of his mind while his officers remained prudently silent, allowing the general's finger to circle a spot on the map.

*

Commander Solomon made the latest assessment of his defences. He had lost 50 of his men, mostly to howitzer fire and the wild bullet that had found its unwary victim. He considered his casualty rate high, considering that the fight had yet to reach the camp. The dead were hastily buried with little ceremony. The war had ended for them, but not for the living. The living had the morrow's problem to handle, and his was the responsibility to ease that problem without a shadow of sentiment.

'They'll be back in the morning, starting with a bombardment. We know the pattern now,' he told his men after the burial.

'They must have lost around 400 men,' a lieutenant projected, 'but they still have a sizeable force.'

'Pity, we can't take the fight to them in the night,' said a lieutenant regretfully. The guerrillas were adept at fighting in the dark. They knew their jungle well, but realized that Solomon would not risk an adventure that would endanger the efficacy of his defensive strengths.

'I think we're done for the day,' he said in a tired voice. 'Get back to your bunkers and patch up what is possible. Also check your ammunition,' he instructed. 'We should be receiving supplies shortly before the moon reaches mid sky.'

Commander Solomon reconnoitred the perimeter, supervising the placement of lookouts and wandered towards the gorge. It was eerie with the silent testimony of the dead that they would never see the rainbow again. A melancholy wormed into his hardened warrior heart at the thought as he strolled back towards the river bank, sighing gloomily as he sat and listened to the rippling flow. He enjoyed the peace and the silence upon the river and was thankful to God that he had lived the day…and as the moon rose high to the midheavens above, he saw a bamboo raft with boxes of ammunition touch the riverbank and unload its lethal stock of sustenance. He strolled back to the bunker, savouring the delightful aroma of pork being cooked in the village, humming to himself an old Karen ballad.

Heaven vast the Eternal placed,
Earth beneath the Eternal placed;
Heaven and earth He cleft apart.
Placed whom when He would depart?
The Eternal ordered Heaven vast,
Fixed the earth's foundation fast;
Heaven and earth asunder cleft,
Man and woman there were left.
Like a top the round earth spinning,
How lived folk on the beginning?
Like thread on reel it circles round,
What have the first folk on it found?
Round the earth spins like a top,
Turned as reel without a stop;

Here the first folk lived at leisure,
Here the first folk lived for pleasure.

But where is the leisure, where is the pleasure? Solomon asked, looking up at the sky.

*

Having studied the map astutely and concluding that there was no track that his troops could take to spring upon the camp from behind, General Sein Lwin began to crystallize an audacious plan that would restore the honour of his rank and the esteem of his troops. He motioned his officers to gather around him for the revelation without a second thought.

'The answer is at the river,' he announced emphatically.

'But that's beyond the Karen camp, sir,' remarked an officer.

'Do you think I'm stupid?' the general bellowed. God, why did he have so many inept officers under his command, he bewailed to himself. He granted that they were all graduates from the academy, but he wished that he had some like the Karens now, practical fighters and not classroom warriors who were good at shooting civilians. He felt ashamed with the perfidious thought and controlled his anger immediately.

'Here,' he announced, pointing at a spot further down the river, 'should be shallow waters. A battalion of our troops will cross the river skirting the hill and get onto land.'

His officers looked askance on hearing the general's words but said nothing, having lost their appetite for another bout of chastisement. They had had enough of the general's bellicosity for the day.

'I know it's Thai territory, but the operation will be quick, and we can race back to our side of the river before the Thais can react,' the general said.

'What do we do if we encounter border guards?' asked a lieutenant colonel in earnest.

'Sensible question, Colonel,' the general commended, feeling that he was getting somewhere at last. 'As usual, they will have few border guards, who can be contained easily. They will not be a threat; the mere size of our troops will intimidate them. Carry some grenade launchers with you,' he ordered, and designated the lieutenant colonel as the officer to lead the operation.

'Now, this is what I plan,' announced the general. 'At about 6:00 am tomorrow morning, we will start a bombardment from here. By that time, you should have positioned your troops across the river behind the Karen camp.'

'I will be there,' answered the lieutenant colonel, having recovered from the dismay a moment ago when the general had chosen him to lead the expedition across the river.

'It shouldn't take you more than, say, three or four hours to be in position, and you should be able to hear the bombardment from there,' the general said. 'Wait for a red flare in the sky at 6:45 am. That will be the signal for your troops to double back across the river and charge the Karen camp from behind.'

'Understood,' acknowledged the lieutenant colonel, swallowing his unease.

'There will be no radio contact of any kind from your side until you are back on our soil,' the general ordered. 'The Thais might stumble onto our frequency.'

'Yes, sir,' replied the lieutenant colonel.

'Good,' observed General Sein Lwin. 'From here, at the same time, we will charge up the gorge, drawing their fire…which I don't think can be much. I expect the continuous barrage from our howitzers would pin them down until the last possible minute.'

'Thank God the mines are gone,' expressed an officer with relief.

'Thank your dead comrades,' snapped General Sein Lwin.

'Ideally, you should have crossed the river when we reach the outer perimeters of their camp,' the general said. 'They will be distracted and their fire will be diverted…and then, gentlemen, we have them in a nutcracker.'

'Excellent plan, sir,' congratulated the officers. They themselves reckoned it to be the only viable solution that offered a military victory and an end to their agony, and shirked their unease with the issue of the violation of the borders of another country. That, they admitted with relief, was the general's responsibility alone. They would merely follow his orders.

'The surprise alone will kill them,' General Sein Lwin concluded gleefully, and clenched his sweaty palms in earnest anticipation. He would teach these Karens some tactics, he promised himself.

'All right, I'll talk to Rangoon and get their approval. Get me the radio,' the general commanded. 'Let's see whether I can swing in a couple of planes to strafe the camp as well.'

*

Military Headquarters
Communications Centre
Yangon

Corporal Kyit Thwe was reading his favourite comic about a Burmese hero—an insuperable army major who consistently defeated his choice adversaries: either the renegade army of Khun Sa in the Shan state or the cowardly Karens hiding in the jungles of the south-east. The Burmese major always prevailed over intense battles, regardless of the difficult terrain, customarily after encountering superior enemy forces behind an abundance of machine-gun nests from which spewed relentless fire that no charging opponent could dream of penetrating. The Burmese major excitedly read the fawning wireless operator, who was in the process of eliminating a series of enemy machine-gun nests all by himself—blazing away with two huge and heavy machine guns that he had wrenched from the turret of a disabled enemy armoured car with his steely hands; the routed enemy beginning to plead for mercy, when the sharp whine of the wireless snapped his heightened imagination from the dramatic climax of the Burmese Rambo's heroics.

'Yes, general. Immediately, sir,' he acknowledged, and dispatched an assistant to fetch General Khin Maung Nyunt. This must be very big and extremely important, he thought, and wished that he was blazing his machine gun at the enemy alongside General Sein Lwin.

'Speak up,' General Khin Maung Nyunt commanded as soon as he entered the wireless room.

'We are on the verge of a victory, sir. The Karens will no longer bother us,' informed the voice on the radio.

'Excellent. Good job done, man,' Khin Maung Nyunt responded. 'Are you attacking Manerplaw?'

'Aah….Not yet, sir, but it is a conceivable certainty,' returned the voice on the other end. 'We're about to crack Hill 4044.'

'That's not bad news at all,' commented Khin Maung Nyunt. 'There's only one other thing that's impeding our immediate termination of the enemy, sir,' the voice on the radio crackled.

'What's that?' enquired Khin Maung Nyunt, suspecting a catch, and began to wonder whether the voice was trying to conceal some kind of a failure.

'In order to seal the fate of the Karens permanently,' whined the voice above the static, 'I would greatly appreciate a token air support, sir.'

'What!' Khin Maung Nyunt exclaimed, alert now that his hunch had been correct. 'Why the aircraft? You're in trouble, aren't you?' Nyunt was averse to deploying aircraft for counter-insurgency operations, especially after the loss of a couple of them recently.

'Just one or two will do. Fly over the camp once and spray the scoundrels to show them who's boss,' the voice on the air wave appealed to.

'Is that all?'

'We have pounded them to smithereens already, and our brave soldiers are repeatedly assaulting the camp despite sustaining severe casualties,' went on the voice, paving the way now to soften the harshness of the truth that the generals in Rangoon would sooner or later get. There was no avoiding the issue.

'How so?' demanded Khin Maung Nyunt, disquieted at the trickle of information he suspected would eventually lead to a dismal picture. He disliked losing a large number of soldiers in any single combat. It was bad for morale.

'The intelligence report was not accurate, sir. There were hundreds of them, nearly matching our strength,' the voice briefed and continued, 'they're using heavy calibre arms that they've never had before and they're actively training our students.'

'How many have you lost?' demanded Khin Maung Nyunt in plain cold anger. He would have a word with Myo Mint, he promised himself.

'Only about one-third our strength, but we got an equal number of them,' prevaricated the voice.

'You fool!' reprimanded Khin Maung Nyunt. 'Only one-third? Why…that's the least you could have done with the artillery I've given you!' He'd have the hide of the man, Khin Maung Nyunt vowed.

'Sir,' the voice remonstrated, 'they're on a steep hill with only a narrow gorge leading to the camp which was mined…and

I'm not exaggerating about the weapons. You can verify that for yourself when I capture this camp.'

The promise of capture of this bastion of defiance mellowed Khin Maung Nyunt. He wanted the fall of this camp desperately. And as army man himself, he did not envy Sein Lwin's task.

'Very well then,' he announced, 'you'll have a couple of our fly boys in the morning over the camp.'

'Sir, 6:00 to 6:15 am, and not later because they'll be strafing us then. Thank you…and there's one more thing,' returned the voice.

'What are you bargaining for now?' asked Khin Maung Nyunt in irritation, fearing that he hadn't heard the worst yet.

'I sincerely want to deliver this camp to you, sir, but I fear that the enemy can still cheat the Tatmadaw from a rightful victory,' replied the voice.

'What are you getting at, man?' growled an aggravated Khin Maung Nyunt.

'There's a river behind the camp and it offers the rascals an ideal escape to Thailand. I want to prevent that. The Thais treat them well, which will help them to stage a fight another day,' the voice of General Sein Lwin came clear across the airwaves.

'What do you propose to do?' asked Khin Maung Nyunt.

'Crossing over quickly and springing back on the camp from the Moei River. There's no other way, but I promise you absolute victory and a termination of the Karen threat for all time,' replied General Sein Lwin.

'Do you know what you're talking about?' demanded Khin Maung Nyunt, taken aback by the audacity of Sein Lwin.

'Yes, sir, I do,' asserted Sein Lwin. 'Otherwise, you'll have an empty camp.'

'Damn,' cursed the general. He loathed being outwitted by the Karens as much as he disapproved of the Thais who granted his enemies refugee status and allowed them to live on their soil. 'Very well,' Khin Maung Nyunt consented after a moment's deliberation, 'but make it lightning quick and don't get caught on the wrong side of the river, because if you do, I will not take responsibility. Do you understand?'

'Yes, sir. Thank you.' The traffic on the airwave was terminated, giving General Sein Lwin the opportunity to implement his military acumen, while the generals in Yangon had found a convenient scapegoat—should one be needed.

*

The Hill
6:00 AM

The whole round earth God came to form,
He can make broad, He can make narrow;
The whole round earth God came to mend,
With ease He can make broad or narrow.
Earth is the sleeping place of God,
Hence noiseless thou, with heel-prints light,
Thy way must take;
Earth is His widely spreading couch, soft-footed steal thou through the night,
Lest He awake.

—a Karen saying

In the soporific quiet of the dawn, the few Karen guards on the river bank had not heard the distant splash of wading feet or the suppressed squelch of muddied boots across the border. Commander Solomon had not considered the callousness or desperation of the Burmese Army, that in order to retrieve victory from abject defeat, they would dare risk an international incident with the Thais. He briefly browsed through an album of stamps a childhood friend had given him a long time ago. He had often wondered what had become of the friend in the land of the Brahmins, and smiled at the memory of the days when they had sung the songs of The Beatles as his calloused fingers coursed through the thick mop of hair he wore again. He didn't know that he wouldn't live through the dawn as he went to sleep that night.

'Solomon! Solomon! Wake up!' cried out the watch as shells from the Burmese artillery exploded in the camp.

'What!' Solomon bolted from the soiled and frayed rug that was his bed and tried to orient himself in the confines of the bunker, shaking the torpor away from himself. He had slipped in deep slumber early in the morning. The explosions continued fiercely and within a few minutes, he realized that something was awfully wrong. The Burmese were firing their guns too early for one; they usually waited until the morning mist had cleared before they tried any assault. He rushed out of the bunker with the safety catch of his automatic rifle off for instant fire.

'Solomon, they're coming!' shouted a startled lieutenant.

'Fire away, give them hell,' he shouted back, and quickly swept his perimeter with the eye of an eagle. The machine-gunners and the mortar men were responding aptly, and the men on the flanks were ready to lob grenades down the hill, should the Burmese troops try outflanking them again. A few more bunkers were blazing, their dead strewn about grotesquely. The Burmese gunners had scored direct hits, he surmised. He must have lost two dozen of his men already, he calculated; some of them while attending to nature's call, he thought, angry at the indignity of it all, and jumped into the lead bunker facing the gorge.

'My God,' gasped the machine-gunner, as a burst of automatic fire ripped his chest, killing him instantly. Solomon discerned immediately that the roof of the bunker had collapsed and most of the protective teak and sandbags blown away, which had exposed the gunner dangerously. To his horror, he saw the other inmates of the bunker dead, their blood oozing from gaping ugly wounds. Another direct hit, he guessed, and saw the rush of the oncoming Burmese soldiers. He grabbed the machine gun and emptied the entire belt into the charging troops, faltering their ranks askew with the avenging bullets.

'The shelling is the heaviest by far,' rasped a guerrilla who jumped in beside him, and then discharged his magazine into the faltering troops.

'We'll have to withdraw,' shouted Solomon above the raucous noise of the guns and pulled the guerrilla away with him, rolling into a fox hole nearby as several shells from the Burmese guns exploded around the bunker they had just vacated.

'Looks like an all-out assault to me,' contended the guerrilla. 'They're throwing everything at us.'

'Let's give them back everything we've got then,' Solomon said in encouragement, and fired his weapon in the direction of the vacated bunker where the charging Burmese troops were grouping.

'We can't hold on here for long,' observed the guerrilla.

'We'll have to regroup and form another defensive line,' concurred Solomon as the troops grouping in front of them charged.

'Use your grenades!' Solomon yelled as he took aim, and fired his automatic while the guerrilla tossed a grenade, following up with another in quick succession.

'Let's fall back now,' Solomon hissed as the grenades detonated.

The guerrilla shadowed Solomon on their serpentine retreat to a bunker in the rear, but as they reached cover, the guerrilla behind Solomon pitched forward in a death roll. He had been cut down by a hail of Burmese bullets.

'Aeroplanes! Aeroplanes!' screamed a frenzied voice as two propeller-driven aircraft—Spitfires Ne Win got from Austria—swooped in low from the west, their coughing guns tacking the damp earth with a mass of human flesh. The Spitfires roared overhead and flew unmolested towards the teak, dipping their wings in salute to their comrades on the ground, who would finish the remnants of resistance in the camp.

Elsewhere in the camp, shells were bursting from the raging guns of the legion in the teak. The Tatmadaw had accelerated its battle tempo and their troops had breached the outer defensive perimeters of the Karens. The guerrillas fought back tenaciously, giving ground little at a time and extracting fearful penalties from the Burmese troops, who inched bloodily ahead. Solomon, in the thick of the bloodletting that was now decimating his camp, realized that the battle would deteriorate very soon to hand-to-hand combat, which would deprive his men of the chance to escape into the dense jungles or across the river. Outnumbered and outgunned, he decided to give the command to disperse when a shrill cry from the river snatched his voice momentarily and paralysed him.

'The river! They're coming from the river!'

The brief moment that benumbed Solomon telescoped into a spell over the camp, a muteness that descended upon Karen guerrilla and Burmese soldier alike until in an instant, their ears rang with the deafening chilling roar of a legion that appeared from the river front, clad in jungle green.

'Fight your way out and disperse,' the recovered voice of Solomon crashed over the hideous roar approaching from the river, triggering the chatter from the guns that had fallen silent for that brief state of suspension in the camp.

The guerrillas had been caught by complete surprise and like the stunned, unsuspecting Thai border guards patrolling the other side of the river at the time, they watched the Burmese troops charging across the river and pouring in to the camp. The Karen defences crumpled swiftly as they fought their way out to disperse into the deep jungles. A symphony of bullets slammed into Solomon, killing him instantly that morning, before he could have tasted his first cup of tea. His camp that had valiantly repulsed repeated onslaughts by the Burmese Army now lay in smouldering ruin. Few escaped the concentrated fire of the soldiers…and the few captured were shot out of hand. The army was not looking for prisoners that morning.

'Burn the bodies,' ordered General Sein Lwin two hours later after inspecting the fallen camp. He kicked about the ruins and was disappointed that the students had escaped him, and felt sorry for his troops that the trophies of victory were denied to them. The women of the camp had disappeared as well. He was surprised, however, with the album of stamps that was found intact in a shattered bunker, and wondered who had the time to be a philatelist in the midst of war.

Mending Fences

Intelligence Headquarters
Bangkok
9:30 AM

The office of General Pawa bustled with nervous energy that morning three hours after the soldiers of General Sein Lwin had crossed back to the safety of their borders. The news had startled him at first, and a few more hours later, his emotions catapulted him to outrage. Telephone bells jangled, dial tones purred while the telex chattered in his office to decipher the morning's incidence at the border. He was in a state of confusion when Lieutenant Colonel Phuphathna entered his office.

'You've no doubt that it's not U Nu's or some other dissident rabble that is responsible?' the general asked.

'No, General,' replied the lieutenant colonel. 'This was no rabble that staged this from our territory and the attack was on a Karen camp, not a Burmese Army base.'

'Fine,' the general nodded. 'That takes care of one thing. We have not exported an overt operation beyond our borders.'

'Which brings us to the fact that the Burmese have violated our borders in order to gain a tactical advantage over their foe,' Lieutenant Colonel Phuphathna commented.

'Which means the fellows in Rangoon know about this,' General Pawa deducted.

'I can't see how not,' the lieutenant colonel agreed with the general.

'This is absolutely deplorable. Any casualty on our side?' the general asked.

'Only a few border guards, I believe,' replied Lieutenant Colonel Phuphathna.

'How can they disrespect the sovereignty of our country? Do they think we're eunuchs!' the incensed general hollered.

'We have to take firm measures, sir. Don't forget, the barbarians have invaded us more than once in our past history,' the lieutenant colonel advised.

'We've also done the same thing with them many times as far as history tells me. Okay, we'll go on an inspection in the afternoon and ask the army chief to accompany us. It will be wise to bolster the presence of our troops at the border to discourage this kind of incident from occurring again,' the general decided. 'They can do it again.'

'Quite right, General. However, I am not afraid of the Burmese attacking us,' the lieutenant colonel said and offered an opinion, saying, 'but I can't put it past them to attack the refugee camps on our territory next.'

'You're right!' observed the general. 'The camps are vulnerable. They can attack it with impunity.'

'We can either move the camps to the interior or have our troops dig in at the border,' the lieutenant colonel said.

'I prefer troops at the border,' commented the general. 'No harm flexing our muscles a bit, eh?'

'Frankly, I prefer that myself,' agreed the lieutenant colonel. 'Our troops need the exercise.'

'Exercise?' queried the general.

'Pardon me for saying so, General,' the lieutenant colonel answered, 'our troops are good at staging our own little coups to decide who will be prime minister and who won't be.'

'Watch it there, Colonel,' hastily chaffed the general.

'Regardless of the facts, sir,' the lieutenant colonel continued, 'we must take into account the political shifts taking place around us now, or we will be helpless like we were during the Cambodia and the Vietnam crisis—not to mention the Laotian to counter any determined aggression.'

'Yes, I see,' General Pawa accepted.

'And of all our neighbours, it's the Burmese who have, yet again, shown little regard to our sovereignty,' concluded Lieutenant Colonel Phuphathna.

'That's correct,' accepted the general. 'Damn their insolence!'

*

SLORC Headquarters
Yangon
Two Days Later

The atmosphere in General Khin Maung Nyunt's office was tense and explosive with the pall of smoke from the general's cheroot hovering hazily, ready to ignite with another puff of recrimination. The Thais had been quick in reacting to the incident at the border, and had issued biting diplomatic protests—worded strongly—to his government. His office had, in turn, issued strong denials which were rejected by the Thais, who were now demanding an official apology and an assurance that such an incident would not occur again. He looked at General Myo Mint sitting across him, and hoped that they could contain the situation before it caused irreparable damage.

'What's the situation at the border now?' General Khin Maung Nyunt asked.

'They've moved in troops and have dug in,' replied Myo Mint.

'Battle ready, I suppose?' the army chief asked sarcastically.

'They've taken it very seriously and have publicized the fact that we are likely to attack the refugee camps on their territory,' responded the intelligence chief.

'I'm aware of that,' the general said. 'They've also claimed responsibility for any refugee on their soil. What I'm wondering is whether we can arrange a flag meeting with their area commander and placate them.'

'How?' enquired the intelligence chief.

'We'll say that it was the work of an overzealous officer who took the decision on his own, and that we will conduct an inquiry,' proposed the general.

'What about the government level?' asked Myo Mint. 'They might insist.'

'Well, if it goes to that…then we will offer a sacrifice,' the general answered.

'Who?'

'Sein Lwin.'

'Fine, I'll get in touch with their intelligence and army chiefs and see whether we can hold a flag meeting of the area commanders,' said the intelligence chief.

'Meanwhile, I'll handle Sein Lwin and his men. They did a marvellous job, don't you think?' the general asked.

'Fine job. The Karens will not be able to rise again as a formidable foe,' acknowledged Myo Mint. 'We can tackle Khun Sa now, after we wipe out Manerplaw.'

'Pity, I'll have to let the Butcher go,' General Khin Maung Nyunt remarked. 'We'll let him disappear into the faceless crowd. We owe him that at least.'

'A fair price for peace, General?' Myo Mint asked with a smile.

'Cheap, actually,' the general said, 'considering that we bagged the Karens.'

'Which reminds me, General,' the intelligence chief said, 'with the Karens out of the picture, our troublemakers have nowhere to go now except Thailand, and I think we should firmly impress upon their government that we do not like the idea of them harbouring dissidents.'

'Yes,' answered the general. 'At the appropriate time, Myo Mint, at the appropriate time. We just cannot afford to upset our plans for Asian membership.'

'What about Aung San Suu Kyi?' Myo Mint asked.

'We'll keep her in unless, of course, she is prepared to be exiled,' replied the general.

'Which she has refused,' reminded the intelligence chief.

'I know,' agreed the general. 'I just can't understand her stubbornness.'

'There is still a rumble in the air, sir,' commented the intelligence chief.

'Let's see for how long,' the general said. 'We can start restricting her husband's visits. No visit by the children either for our sister. Let's see how much of a mother she is. As a wife, she's put her ambition beyond her husband.'

'We are getting a lot of adverse press, you know,' Myo Mint remarked.

'As long as it's press, it's all right,' shrugged the general. 'In the meantime, let's get ahead with the national reconciliation programme as speedily as possible. Let's start talking to the monks and promise them renovation of their beloved shrines. We'll start with the Shwedagon in Yangon. Let us also start restoring our ancient heritage of Pagan and Mandalay, and any other that will stimulate national interest and keep the scribes and scholars busy.

It's about time that they earned their livelihood. That should take care of the religious and cultural aspects of our society.'

'What about the educational institutions?' enquired the intelligence chief.

'The best thing is to start honouring scholastic brilliance by giving away dazzling prizes to outstanding students, which will only ensure their allegiance to our regime. It will also help us catch the delinquents amongst them,' replied the general.

'Excellent policy,' commented the intelligence chief.

'We have got to improve upon the past, don't we?' asked the general.

'Yes, of course,' complied Myo Mint.

'Which also means that while we, the regime, work along those lines, you cannot default on you tasks ahead,' reminded Kin Maung Nyunt.

'Yes, of course. How can I?' acknowledged the intelligence chief, envying the general and his new junta and its glamorous path to public relations, while he would have to continue with his unpleasant and dirty task—the demolition of Aung San Suu Kyi and her party.

*

In early 1996, the Burmese government invited a plane-load of Thai dignitaries, ostensibly to mend ties that have deteriorated since the border violation. An impressive red-carpet welcome is accorded to the delegates. Schoolchildren lined the route chosen for the motorcade, waving little flags of friendship in their little coerced hands.

The Burmese government then declared 1996 as 'Visit Myanmar Year'.

The regime energetically pursued avenues of procuring foreign investments, but Aung San Suu Kyi declared adamantly that foreign investments would only strengthen the regime while the common man would not benefit.

Change of the Guard

India
Post 1995–2015

The fall of the Karen camps and their headquarters (HQ), Manerplaw, to the Burmese Army had been summarily reported in the international press, and had dismayed Simon as much as the news of the continued quarantine of Aung San Suu Kyi in her ancestral home. Would the Karens ever find a voice again, or would they mutate genetically into other races as their cry for an identity disappear in the wilderness of humanity, he wondered.

The same sense of hopelessness was felt by his mother, for one day, she said, 'Simon, when I die, I want to be buried next to your father.' She had, on an earlier occasion, expressed a wish to be buried next to her mother.

There was no more talk of visiting Burma now, nor was there any hope of Aung San Suu Kyi's early triumph over a regime harder than Ne Win's.

The SLORC had mutated into the State Peace and Development Council (SPDC) in 1997 with General Than Shwe, still Ne Win's man, at the helm. Trained in psychological warfare, the general had attended a special course for army officers in the Soviet Union run by the *KGB. Rising from instructor at the Army HQ, he rose from company commander* to *battalion commander and, finally, to general and commander-in-chief* of *the Burmese Army on 18 March 1990, and that of the armed forces in 1992.*

But the new junta seemed prepared for the return to democracy, provided there were power-sharing arrangements with the NLD—including guaranteed immunity from prosecution for past human rights abuses.

Aung San Suu Kyi was not inclined. After her release in 1995, she was again placed under house arrest in September 2000.

*

'It's another world out there for the Karens, Mom,' Simon tried consoling his ageing mother who was ailing from a heart disease. 'That world is as distant from us as democracy is to the Burmese, except that we live without the fear of the midnight knock which is the reward for the price that we have paid. They don't have that, despite the price they have paid, and it appears to me that they will have to pay more.'

'I hope Aung San Suu Kyi prevails in the end,' his mother said. 'At least the next generation can learn the meaning of decency and know what it is to be free from fear. I hope she doesn't give up.'

'Unless they deport her on some ground, the indications are that she won't. Burma is under the microscope now and she has become too prominent to be ignored. At best, they can only malign her and resort to something more drastic, like depriving her of visits of her sons even after her husband died,' Simon remarked.

'Yes, it will be very interesting to see what will happen now,' his mother agreed.

'Global politics has changed, Mom,' Simon commented. 'The United States does not have to contend with the USSR simply because it doesn't exist anymore. Vietnam's a thing of the past and so is Cambodia, which means the Americans can have better latitude if they want to turn their attention to this part of the world if they wished.'

'The Burmese still have a few friends, don't they?' Dora commented. 'Japanese aid for one.'

'Yes. Keeping in with world opinion, the Japanese, too, would have to re-evaluate their philosophy of aid to the Burmese sooner or later. China's busy with Hong Kong since 1997 and is building trade relations with the Americans. They're more interested in making money now.'

'With all this happening, I don't see where the chaps in Rangoon will find an ally, and Fidel's too far away,' Simon postulated. 'The fact is that they've pulled out of all power blocks, political and economic, and are pretty much isolated at the moment.'

'They could try to worm their way into one,' observed Dora.

'Which one? That's the big question! India probably is not in their calculation. It will be China and North Korea, and when they do, it will give them more power to deal with Aung San Suu Kyi and that will be a tragedy,' he said.

'Let's wait and see,' his mother said in resignation as the family sat down to a meal.

Own know kow swe! (The delight of the family and new friends!)

Dora's mind now grappled with the reality that, for the remaining years of her life, she might not see the change that she so wanted in the land of her birth.

'I can see that Aung San Suu Kyi and the NLD will require a lot more support than they are getting now in Burma, and from the international community,' she observed.

'Not just political verbiage but a unified, strong international will that would complement a cadre of hardcore volunteers in the country who will brave death—which I can't see happening yet,' Simon added.

'Yes, there seems to be no other way,' she agreed.

'Unless, of course, Aung San Suu Kyi works with the generals for a solution,' Simon flippantly said.

'How?' asked Dora.

'Well,' explained her son, suppressing the urge to laugh out loud, 'she tells the generals, "enough is enough…things have got out of hand, *sayas* (master or sir). I realize I've knocked a little too hard on your heads and I'm sorry. So let's have a tête-à-tête. Declare that the mission of the SLORC in the country has been accomplished and that it's now safe for the SPDC to hand over the government of the country to me. After all, I won the elections, you know. Now, I promise I won't disturb you boys. You can retain your privileges and I'll make a provision for it in the new Constitution. I'll still need an army, you know, and you chaps are the army; seasoned and well-trained and all that."'

'They're not going to believe her,' she interrupted.

'Wait, Mom,' Simon ignored the interruption. 'The best part is when she says to them… "Okay, you don't believe me? No problem. If I fail to make good my promise anyway, all you've got to do is stage another coup and that shouldn't be a problem; you guys have enough experience in such matters already."'

The members of the family laughed and Dora laughed as well, and she laughed heartily until her eyes brimmed with tears. She hadn't had a good laugh in a long time. Then, the laughter died and she observed despondently, 'In the meantime, the Karens might disappear as a race.'

'Unless the world lends them an ear, I'm afraid they might end up as the faceless Cambodians in Thailand—a diaspora forever doomed to be aliens and refugees,' Simon said helplessly.

He thought of the guerrillas on the south-eastern hill tracks of Burma, bordering Thailand, and wondered how many of them he knew as a boy in Rangoon would be amongst them—or for that matter, how many of them could have died fighting in their desperation to derive some meaning from their existence. He wondered about his boyhood friend, Solomon…and beyond the realm of imagination, could not picture any certainty. It had been over 20 years since he last received a letter. He wasn't even sure that they would recognize each other if destiny were to chance a meeting between them.

'The Karens have a better chance with Aung San Suu Kyi, and I hope that she doesn't give up,' said Dora and looked at her children and their families, and wondered whether there would be one of them to visit the country in the future. She recognized that, except for the youngest who had been a baby when they left Burma, any discussion on the subject had sparked in them vague impressions of their early childhood in the land of their birth.

'I cannot disagree with that, Mom. And as you said, let's wait and see. That's the only thing we can do at the moment,' Simon nodded, signalling to his brothers and sisters that the discussion of the painful subject was at an end for the evening. But he knew that unconsciously, their Burma watch would tick, audible now…but soon would become a distant fading:

Gloan Na Na Gloan Na na
Too Ley Ley au Ley, Too Ley Ley au Ley
Too Lay Lay au Lay
Too Ley au Ley Too Ley Ley au Ley
Gloan Na Na Gloan Na Na…

Dora died in December 2000, three days after Christmas.

Naypyidaw

On 7 March 2002, Ne Win and his daughter Sandar were placed under house arrest in Rangoon. Sandar's husband and three sons were taken into custody for allegedly plotting to kidnap General Than Shwe with two other colleagues, and hold them at Ne Win's home until they agreed to reorganize the government to suit Ne Win's future plans.

Ne Win died on 5 December, and General Than Shwe no longer needed to contend with anyone.

Aung San Suu Kyi was placed under house arrest again in May 2003.

Abandoned by the SPDC, the Butcher died on 12 April 2004 in acute poverty.

On 27 March 2006, over 12,000 troops marched in the new capital Naypyidaw for a massive military parade to mark Burma's Armed Forces Day—the anniversary of the 1945 uprising against the Japanese occupation of Burma. Names of townships in development were all derived from ancient Indian Pali.

August 2007 saw protesters again on the streets of Burma after the junta raised the price of cooking gas by 500 per cent and doubled the cost of transport fuels. The movement gained momentum and became known as the Saffron Revolution. Buddhist monks had joined in, leading it. It was the largest protest seen in Burma since 1988. Hundreds of protesters led by thousands of monks marched in Rangoon.

The junta cracked down. Than Shwe ordered the soldiers 'shoot to kill'.

Than Shwe then finalized the Constitution, giving ultimate power to the army commander-in-chief, sequestering 25 per cent of the seats in the parliament to unelected military appointees.

Burma, under Ne Win's Tatmadaw, underwent a dark period when it was suspicious of everyone and abused all equally in its bloodlust. Under Than Shwe, the situation got darker. After the military rout of the Karens, Naypyidaw turned towards the Rohingyas of the Rakhine State.

British colonial policies had encouraged migrant labour from Bengal, India, to settle in the Arakan region of Burma, bordering what is now Bangladesh. This was for rice cultivation and profits. Many Muslims entered Burma—the Muslim population tripled to a million, living alongside the Yakines or Rakhines. The British promised these Muslims—who became the Rohingyas—separate land in exchange for support. During the Second World War, the Rohingyas sided with the British, while Myanmar's nationalists supported the Japanese.

The Arakan was a front line where the Muslim Rohingyas fought with the British, while the Yakine Buddhist nationalists joined forces with the Japanese. Muslims and Buddhists attacked each other, leading to massacres on both sides between 1942 and 1943—just like it happened between the Burmese and the Karens. Following the war, the British rewarded the Rohingyas with prestigious government posts but not with an autonomous state.

After Burma's independence in 1948, some of the Rohingyas in Arakan rebelled against U Nu's government for an autonomous state. Most Rohingyas did not, and some religious leaders even condemned the religious justifications used by the rebels. However, the rebels' demands were shared by many, including recognition as indigenous Burmese peoples and rejection of Buddhist claims that Burmese Muslims were outsiders. The rebels also demanded that Muslims be integrated into the Burmese government and army, and improve the economy and education in Arakan. When talks with the government failed, the rebel guerrilla forces drove Buddhists out of villages in Arakan. The Burmese Army responded by razing Muslim villages and mosques.

Ne Win's military coup in 1962 ended formal Muslim and all other minority political activity, which was seen as a threat to Burmese national identity.

In 1978, Ne Win's Tatmadaw launched a military operation called Nagamin (Dragon King), and began screening the population and registration of foreigners. More than 200,000 Rohingyas fled to Bangladesh, amid allegations of army abuses. The army denied wrongdoing of any kind. This operation forced relocation of Muslim villagers, and was accompanied by widespread looting, rape, arson and the desecration of mosques.

Between 1991 and 1992, in response to the increasing fighting capability of the Rohingya Solidarity Organization (RSO), the SLORC's overture was Operation Pyi Thaya (Clean and Beautiful Nation), to expel 'foreigners' and Rohingya insurgents (specifically of the RSO) from the area. It resulted in the displacement of another 200,000 to 250,000 ethnic people, but failed to prevent further attacks by the RSO, which continued until the end of the 1990s.

*

On 25 July 2010, General Than Shwe, ostensibly on a religious pilgrimage, arrived in India. He began his five-day visit starting his tour at Bodh Gaya, its earlier Pali name Bodhimanda-Vihara, where the Mahabodhi temple is situated. It was here that Gautama

Siddhartha, sitting under the Bodhi tree, attained enlightenment. He then went to several Buddhist temples in Kushinagar. Was it his quest for enlightenment or to remind his host of Pagan's first Bamar king Anawratha's ascendancy over the ancient Pyu and Mon kingdoms, whose culture originated in India? Or was it to strengthen ties between Burma and India before a storm brewing ahead?

Aung San Suu Kyi was still under house arrest.

However, in Gaya, the general was greeted by activists with posters accusing him of crimes against humanity. Scores of pro-democracy campaigners demonstrated in New Delhi, accusing the general of ordering the ruthless crushing of a pro-democracy Saffron Revolution led by monks in 2007, the exploitation of forced labour and a systematic repression of basic human rights on a daily basis.

Unperturbed, the general then held talks with the Indian government, signing agreements on economic cooperation, drug smuggling and terrorist activities across the India–Burma border.

In 2012, sectarian violence erupted again across nine townships in the Rakhine State, displacing another 35,000 people—mostly Muslims. Human Rights Watch reported that the attacks against Rohingya and Muslim communities, in general, were organized, incited, and committed by local Yakine political party operatives, Buddhist monkhood and lay Yakine, visibly supported by state security forces. Rohingya men, women and children were killed, many buried in mass graves and their villages and neighbourhoods razed to the ground.

In 2015, Aung San Suu Kyi was released from house arrest that she was on since November 2010, and won a monumental victory in a general election held on 8 November. The NLD won an absolute majority of seats in both houses of the parliament, placing her in a position where she could govern the country. The military was stupefied. In their conviction of triumph, foreign observers were allowed. Regardless, the military held the defence, home affairs and border affairs ministries, and retained the veto over constitutional change as well as the right to place the country under martial law at any time.

Dowsing her elated spirits surging from such a pinnacle of success for which she had endured so much pain, sacrificing her husband and children, salvoes of dissent, louder than Sein Lwin's, crashed on her. November 2016 saw a major resurgence in the Arakan. On the morning of 25 August 2017, the Arakan Rohingya Salvation Army launched coordinated attacks on 24 police posts and the 552nd Light Infantry Battalion army base in Rakhine State.

Aung San Suu Kyi knew that she was walking a tight rope between the Tatmadaw and the Ethnic Armed Forces, who continue holding unbending positions. Unless the attrition begins hurting both sides and brings about a stalemate which could only hurt more, a genuine negotiation can never be achieved.

Real power still resides with the military in Burma, in control of the state's entire security apparatus.

For the Nobel Laureate, the country's problems do not stop with the Rohingyas. There has been no conclusive settlement with the Shan, Karen, Kachin and other ethnic groups. Armed conflict continues, and hundreds of thousands remain displaced. Human rights abuses—including arbitrary detention, land confiscation, rape and torture continue in the name of development.

The country is yet far from being 'Aung San's Burma'.

Meanwhile, Naypyidaw watches.

Acknowledgements

I thank my wife Christine for her patience and the stream of hot black coffee until the early morning hours, and seeing to it that I did not fall off my chair, which helped me finish this book.

To my surviving brother and sisters, thank you for the faith.

My thanks go to Esha Beteille for her guidance as to where I could go with my manuscript.

I also thank my publisher Niyogi Books, and specially Dr Nirmal Kanti Bhattacharjee for taking up my work and transforming it into this publication.

And not in the least, I thank Vibha Kumar for her deft editing of the manuscript. I have benefitted enormously from her erudition.